VILLA DES ROSES

Willem Elsschot (pseudonym of Alfons de Ridder, 1882–1960), was a major and immensely popular twentieth-century Flemish novelist whose works have the status of classics in both Flanders and the Netherlands. Born in Antwerp, he completed a course in business studies and worked abroad for some years before returning home and eventually establishing an advertising agency in his native city. His first novel, *Villa des Roses* (1913), a tragi-comedy of manners acted out almost entirely within the confines of a small Paris board-ing-house, enjoyed immediate success, particularly in the Netherlands. It was followed after the First World War by *Een ont-goocheling (A Disillusionment)* and *De verlossing (Redemption)*. When Elsschot issued *Lijmen (Soft Soap)* through an unknown Antwerp publisher, it passed largely unnoticed, which discouraged him from writing for nearly a decade. However, his later short novels, includ-ing *Kaas* (*Cheese*, 1933), *Tsjip* (*Chirp*, 1934), *Het been* (*The Leg*, 1938) and *Het dwaallicht* (*Will-o'-the-Wisp*, 1946) established him as a sophisticated stylist and a unique voice in Flemish realism.

Paul Vincent taught Dutch language and literature for many years at London University before becoming a full-time translator in 1989. He has translated various Dutch prose writers, including Harry Mulisch, Helga Ruebsamen, J. Bernlef and H. M. van den Brink.

Villa des Roses

WILLEM ELSSCHOT

Translated with an introduction and notes by
PAUL VINCENT

Granta Books
London • New York

Granta Publications, 2/3 Hanover Yard, Noel Road,
London N1 8BE
This edition published in Great Britain by Granta Books 2003

First published in Great Britain by Penguin Books 1992
First published in the Netherlands 1913

A CIP catalogue record for this book is available from the British
Library.

3 5 7 9 10 8 6 4 2

Set in Plantin by M Rules
Printed and bound in Great Britain by
Mackays of Chatham plc

Dedicated in gratitude to Miss Anna Christina van der Tak,
a loyal friend

Contents

Introduction

The sole reason I write is to produce classic prose, which is beautiful and will stay beautiful. It is pure vanity.

'In reading a book one must be able to say from the very first page that it is by *that* writer and no one else.' For Dutch readers of his compact *œuvre*, Elsschot's criterion of instant recognizability is certainly achieved. His uniqueness has been defined by one commentator as 'above all a tone, a timbre, an attitude, whose complexity makes up for the poverty of the characters and the paucity of ideas'.

Two questions pose themselves: can the unique 'ring' of Elsschot's prose be approximated in translation and, if so, does that constitute all that *Villa des Roses* and the rest have to offer readers without Dutch? As to the first question, the precise modulations of the original certainly pose great problems for the translator, and an eminent critic and admirer warns the unwary: 'The moment the translator starts embellishing, the Elsschot effect disappears.' That effect is achieved variously by extreme succinctness, sometimes brutal and/or ironic (the narrator's senile mother in *Kaas* is described as 'a guttering lamp threatening a farewell explosion'), and by a deadpan, often quasi-biblical solemnity (the disproportionate gravity of 'A silence fell over Flanders' gives epic and comic resonance to a pause in a telephone conversation in the story *Lijmen*). For some further examples, see the discussion of *Villa des Roses* below.

Any answer to the second question requires a context.

Willem Elsschot is the pseudonym of Alfons Jozef de Ridder (1882–1960), who was born and raised in the Flemish port of Antwerp, the son of a prosperous baker. At school his enthusiasm for Dutch and other literature was fired by a gifted teacher, Pol de

Mont (1857–1931), himself a writer and political activist. Besides Balzac, Flaubert and the Flemish poet Guido Gezelle (1830–99), whom he hails as 'a second Virgil', Elsschot's lifelong favourites included such classics of protest and irreverent humour as the medieval poem of Reynard the Fox, the poetry of François Villon (1431–63?) and Joost van den Vondel (1587–1679), and the virtuoso writing of Multatuli (pseudonym of Eduard Douwes Dekker, 1820–87), author of the colonial novel *Max Havelaar* (1860).[1] For Elsschot, Multatuli was a Promethean figure who had held aloft 'the torch of non-conformism and rebellion' and deserved the veneration of the whole Dutch-speaking world.

Expelled from school at the age of sixteen for unruly behaviour, Elsschot flirted with Tolstoyan and anarchist ideas, played the Bohemian and published some derivative Impressionist poetry which he subsequently disowned. A contemporary portrait shows a pale, intense face surmounted by a broad-brimmed hat, the kind that later, in the novel *Lijmen* (*Soft Soap*), is abandoned by its owner Laarmans on forsaking youthful idealism for the world of business. In 1901 the subject of that portrait returned, ostensibly at least, to the path of convention by enrolling at Antwerp Business College. After graduating in 1904 and working in Paris, Rotterdam and Brussels, he finally set up his own Antwerp-based advertising agency in 1931 and continued it until his death.

Elsschot's literary activity, never his main means of livelihood, was limited and spasmodic. A number of striking poems written between 1902 and 1910 were not published until the 1930s. Apart from these he produced a handful of occasional poems, the last of which, a scathing condemnation of the execution of a militant Flemish politician for collaboration in 1946, scandalized the intellectual establishment and was the immediate cause of Elsschot's subsequent near-silence as a writer. He produced a small amount of journalism as the temporary Antwerp correspondent of a Rotterdam daily after the First World War.

However, his classic status in the Low Countries derives largely

---

1   An English translation by Roy Edwards was published in Penguin Classics (1987).

from his eleven novellas, of which *Villa des Roses* (written in 1910 and published in the Netherlands in 1913) is the first. This début, incorporating elements from the author's period of employment in Paris, was followed by *Een ontgoocheling* (*A Disillusionment*, 1921), in which a father's social ambitions for his son are thwarted, and in the same year by *De verlossing* (*Redemption*). The latter story, which focuses on the confrontation between a village priest and a rebellious grocer, and the grocer's daughter's subsequent attempt to redeem her dead father's soul, is Elsschot's only book with a rural setting. It is also the only one in which 'big' political themes (the power of the Catholic Church and the aristocracy in Flanders) are central to the action. As a narrative, it loses some momentum after the climactic scene in which the dying grocer shoots his adversary.

Lijmen (*Soft Soap*, 1924) is the first work to draw on the author's professional experience in the advertising business and arguably his first masterpiece. It features the recruitment or, better, moral seduction of the disillusioned idealist Frans Laarmans by the business guru Boorman, whom Laarmans then assists in foisting thousands of copies of an advertising magazine on a small lift-making firm. Boorman sums up his predatory credo to his acolyte, whom he has rechristened with the exotic name of Teixeira de Mattos, in a memorable mock sermon:

> Vanity, that's the cause of it all, de Mattos. Everyone wants to be Number One, or at least wants to make everyone else think so . . . I drop in on them, one after the other, as the colossal director of the colossal *World Review* . . . Try and believe what you tell them is the truth, then your story sounds all the more convincing. You have to sound convincing. If you are, you can talk a hard-hearted miser into an extravagance that he'll probably shudder at the thought of an hour later. Once I had a bank manager properly warmed up, and I didn't realize it. He had one of those stupid faces that stays blank all the time. Suddenly he reached boiling point. He jumped up, he banged on the table, and he ordered a million copies with an article about his bank. Every family in Belgium must have a copy, he was yelling. He looked like a crusader who'd just caught sight of Jerusalem. But when I hesitated, because I didn't think I could

risk a million copies with that piddling little printer of mine, he came out of his trance and had me marched to the door.

Never be discouraged, even if you have weeks of bad luck. Don't trust in God, de Mattos. Be polite to your clients, because they're your enemies, and don't forget it. They'll only give you what you can wring out of them, and not a cent more.[2]

The so-called *World Review* consists of vacuous paeans of praise to various businesses constructed by Boorman from all-purpose formulae, and was based on the actual *Revue générale illustrée*, of which the author and his partner, in the best truth-is-stranger-than-fiction tradition, sold 100,000 copies to a convent.

Boorman, the embodiment of commercial ruthlessness, in whom some critics have detected traits of the Nietzschean 'superman', Svengali and even Mephistopheles, reappears in later works. His counterpart, Frans Laarmans, the born underdog with Walter Mitty-like aspirations and a troubled conscience, also reappears as the central figure in three subsequent tales. This ambivalent look at business ethics was Elsschot's first book to be published exclusively in Flanders, and received less critical attention than its predecessors.

Elsschot published nothing for the next eight years until his cause was taken up by the Dutch literary magazine *Forum*, whose literary preference was for the non-rhetorical. Elsschot's narratives, described by the poet Martinus Nijhoff as being like 'oblique conversations' with the reader, had obvious appeal. A selection of his earlier poetry, combining traditional form with directness of statement, was published in *Forum*'s first issue, and two writers associated with the magazine, Menno ter Braak and especially Jan Greshoff, encouraged Elsschot to write more fiction.

The first product of his reawakened creativity was *Kaas* (*Cheese*, 1933), in which Laarmans's ambition to leave the drudgery of menial office work and become a successful cheese salesman ends in fiasco, but also in self-acceptance and a return to the bosom

2   Quoted from Willem Elsschot, *Three Novels: Soft Soap/The Leg/Will-o'-the Wisp* (see Further Reading). Unless otherwise stated, translations from Dutch are my own (tr.).

of the family. ('Sweet, darling children. Dear, dear wife,' the book concludes, not wholly ironically.) The cheese trade acts as a metaphor for advertising: 'because publicity was too abstract a subject to write about I chose cheese. It has a shape, a smell and sometimes stinks. I could equally well have chosen fish.' Its dedicatory poem, introduction and list of characters and 'elements' give it a more literary 'packaging' than its predecessors.

A later sequel to *Lijmen*, *Het been* (*The Leg*, 1938), was dedicated to ter Braak. *Tsjip* (*Chirp*, 1934) and its sequel *De leeuwentemmer* (*The Lion-Tamer*, 1938) are the most closely autobiographical of his books, and in them the narrator is reconciled with life by his young grandson after his daughter's marriage to and subsequent divorce from a Pole. *Pensioen* (*Pension*, 1937) involves a mother's elaborate swindle, while *Het tankschip* (*The Tanker*, 1942), though planned as the first in a series of books set in the Second World War, was to remain Boorman's last appearance, as the instigator of a dubious shipping deal.

Het dwaallicht (*Will-o'-the-Wisp*, 1946) has the greatest unity of theme, action and narrative of all the books and perhaps comes closest to the author's stated Flaubert-like ideal of a story 'with a minimum of content and a maximum of tension'. Narrated by Laarmans himself, it describes his abortive search of the Antwerp docks one rainy evening with three Afghan sailors for an address they have been given by a girl called Maria. As they wander in search of the girl, they talk and Laarmans revises his initial prejudices. The odyssey ends with Laarmans's return home to domestic routine, despite the temptation to pursue the quest (with its religious as well as sexual overtones) for himself. The mood of reluctant conformism is encapsulated in the poem 'Marriage', written thirty-six years earlier and published in 1932:

> . . . giving dreams their head
> raises both practical and legal snags,
> and puzzlingly, one's spirit always flags
> in the evenings when it's time for bed.

It was not for nothing that the novelist Simon Vestdijk likened this poem to a miniature novella.

Belated official recognition came after 1945. Elsschot was awarded literary prizes in 1947, 1951 and, posthumously, in 1960. His *Collected Works* appeared in 1957, the first of many editions, and his readership and influence grew steadily, especially in the Northern Netherlands. Himself a lifelong speaker of Antwerp dialect, Elsschot produced a literary idiom which, while not antiseptic or neutral, aims at supra-regional clarity, unlike the admired Gezelle and contemporaries like Stijn Streuvels and Felix Timmermans, who made a virtue of the Flemishness of their language in opposition to the Dutch of the Netherlands.

Elsschot was not a high-profile man of letters and made relatively few pronouncements on his own work or on literature in general. One photograph shows his study as almost bare of books apart from Shakespeare and the Bible (his particular preference was for Ecclesiastes and Job), and he was supposedly reduced on occasion to borrowing copies of his own works from his children. The non-literary image cultivated by the author and some commentators should not, however, be exaggerated. Where he does express himself directly (in his introduction to *Kaas*, his postscript to *Tsjip* and in a number of interviews), he has telling things to say about style in general:

> ... closely allied to music, which developed from the human voice, a vehicle of rejoicing and lamentation long before words on paper were thought of.

> Right from the opening (for a book is a song) one must keep the final chord in mind, and something of it should be interwoven through the whole story like a leitmotif through a symphony ...[3]

3 Such statements bring Elsschot surprisingly close, in tone if not in essence, to the defence of 'pure poetry' by his fellow-townsman, the modernist poet and critic Paul van Ostaijen 1896–1928) in his essay 'Gebruiksaanwijzing der lyriek' ('Lyrical Poetry: Directions for Use', 1927; English version in Paul van Ostaijen, *The First Book of Schmoll*, Amsterdam: Bridges Books, 1982), though there is no evidence that the two ever met or knew each other's work.

In nature, tragedy resides in the things that actually happen. In art, it is more a matter of style than of what actually happens. A herring can be depicted tragically, even though there is nothing intrinsically tragic about such a creature. On the other hand it is not sufficient to say 'My poor father is dead' to achieve a tragic effect . . .

He makes the following comment on his own working method, once described as the 'art of leaving out':

I usually write the whole story right through to the end. The only thing that concerns me is the idea that I am trying to depict, so that I never know in advance what kind of plot there will be. Once the story has been written out the real work starts. I scrap a lot and always try to find the most graphic expression.

The urge to write is seen as an affliction:

My literary work is certainly not a relaxation, more a periodic torture that I cannot escape from. It's like malaria, a three-day fever that lays one low from time to time.

and the artistic vocation as a betrayal of the artist's family:

May my wife and children forgive me for forsaking them for one last time for that accursed realm of splendour where a golden bird sings, far higher than the lark.

Elsschot's relatively small literary output has been attributed to a variety of factors. Professional and family commitments weighed heavily on him, and there was a discouraging lack of recognition for his work, especially between 1924 and 1934. Though his first books were quite well received critically, they made no great impact, and certainly not in Flanders, where the tone was set by the earthy rural epics of Stijn Streuvels (1871–1969) and the folksy exuberance of works like *Pallieter* (1916) by Felix Timmermans (1886–1947); in the Netherlands he was overshadowed by the sophistication and expansiveness of such novelists as Louis Couperus (1863-1923). Last but not least, there is Elsschot's perfectionism, combined with a conviction that creation is an organic process which cannot be forced: 'In art there are no prizes for effort. Don't try to swear if you are not angry or cry if your soul is dry, or rejoice if you aren't full of joy. If there is a genuine pregnancy, birth will follow automatically in its own good time.'

Elsschot's style has been variously characterized as corrosive, cynical, sick, sardonic, stiff and official. This does not, however, preclude a powerful undercurrent of emotion, which the reader feels even without the knowledge that the author frequently wept on reading his work aloud. The emotion is raw and brutal in poems like the previously quoted 'Marriage':

> Perceiving how the creeping mists of age
> had left the sparkle in his wife's eyes quenched,
> her cheeks all worn, her forehead deeply trenched,
> he turned away and fumed in helpless rage . . .

Elsschot expressed the modest hope that 'if my poems are a little prosaic, I hope that on the other hand I have instilled some poetry into my prose.'

Villa des Roses, written in either two or three weeks (the interviews disagree), cannot be denied its share of poignant effect, for example in its use of imagery. The aged Madame Gendron shuffles around coughing like a plague victim ringing a bell, the dying Brizard collapses 'like a snowman that has had boiling water poured over it', Mademoiselle de Kerros's hair 'looked as though it could be ground to dust like saffron between one's fingers', the dying monkey raises its arms aloft 'like the damned in hell'. Black humour and compassion are present in equal measure. In other cases, understatement is used with shocking directness. 'It was a simple funeral,' the narrator coolly observes as the foetus of Louise's aborted child is thrown over a back fence.

However, if measured by the austere standards of the mature Elsschot ('what is not necessary will be excluded and when one character will do a crowd of them is superfluous'), it is almost profligate with its effects, presenting us with an international gallery of characters, perhaps one-dimensional but, like the Brulots and Mademoiselle Kerros, unforgettable, and a succession of incidents, hilarious or gruesome and sometimes both (Madame Dumoulin embroidering in the Bibliothèque Nationale, or Madame Gendron flirting with the corpse of Brizard). The maid Louise, the nearest the action comes to a main character apart from the Villa itself, first appears on the scene only in the fifth chapter.

The authorial tone of this naturalistic study of a run-down Paris boarding-house and the mostly inconsequential lives of its denizens seems more detached than that of the involved personal narrator (Laarmans) of *Lijmen* or *Kaas*, but the microcosm evoked never becomes simply a grotesque freak show. Losers like Louise, Brizard and Marie are more sympathetic than the brash and ambitious 'winner' Grünewald. The (autobiographically based) affair between Louise and Grünewald is the only full treatment of sexual love in Elsschot; elsewhere we find either married routine (*Kaas*) or un-focused longing (*Het dwaallicht*). The philanderer's casually sexist cruelty is mercilessly evoked.

The book is unencumbered by the descriptive excesses of much Dutch Naturalist writing: here the outer and inner reality of the characters is central. Sparing but effective use is made of the Flaubertian device of indirect free style to bring the reader closer to the thoughts of Louise, as in her final bleak perception that she is back home: 'It was her village sure enough.'

One aspect of *Villa des Roses* not much commented on is its use of typographical effects, as in the boarding-house sign, Madame Dumoulin's birthday menu, various bills, the list of Madame Brulot's endearments for Chico and even extracts from a railway timetable. These realistic details provide a certain theatricality as well as 'authen-ticity', and may even faintly recall the typographical experiments of the previously mentioned Paul van Ostaijen. But their presence can probably be interpreted more plausibly as a link with the commercial advertising copy that Elsschot–De Ridder wrote for a living.

Elsschot's great champion, Greshoff, called it 'one of the few masterpieces of [Dutch] realism': 'The right kind of realism is able to intensify and deepen all human actions, imbuing them with a universal significance without sacrificing their links with everyday reality.' Hopefully today's readers of this translation will not find that an empty claim.

Translator's Note

Elsschot's Dutch text is liberally interspersed with French words or phrases, whose function seems to be mostly to add local colour, as well as two songs in French. Not wishing to encumber the text unduly I have kept explanatory notes to a minimum. Three solutions have been variously adopted: where partially or fully explained immediately after their occurrence (as, for example, in Madame Dumoulin's birthday menu), words/phrases have been retained in French, italicized or in upper case (song titles have not been translated); the text of songs, greetings, expletives, etc., when first used, has been translated in the endnotes; in other cases, the French text has been replaced without annotation by an English version. There are a few instances where simple words or phrases, such as *bonjour* or *nom de Dieu*, have been neither translated nor annotated.

The few words of German included by Elsschot, where their meaning is not clear from the context, have mostly been translated in the notes, as has the solitary Latin phrase.

Further Reading

The text used is that of Willem Elsschot, *Verzameld werk* (Amsterdam: P. N. van Kampen en Zoon N.V., 1957).

A selection of previously uncollected work appeared under the title *Zwijgen kan niet verbeterd worden*, ed. A. Kets-Vree (Amsterdam/ Borsbeek: Loeb & Van der Velden/Baart, 1979).

Three of Elsschot's later novels appeared in English in one volume, translated by Alex Brotherton, as *Three Novels: Soft Soap/The Leg/Will-o'-the-Wisp* (Leyden/London/New York: Sijthoff/ Heinemann/ London House & Maxwell, 1965).

On Elsschot and other Dutch-language writers mentioned, see R. P. Meijer, *Literature of the Low Countries* (Cheltenham: Stanley Thornes, 1978).

Villa des Roses

I

Monsieur and Madame Brulot

The Villa des Roses, where the Brulots served meals and let rooms, was in the rue d'Armaillé, an unimposing street in the otherwise spaciously laid out Quartier des Ternes.[1] And what applied to the street applied equally to the house; it was only two storeys high, while the whole district was full of buildings with five or six floors, which towered above the Villa on either side. This gave the boarding-house something of the look of a country house, surrounded and hemmed in by the surging tide of the metropolis. But no one had ever come up with an acceptable explanation for the descriptive tag 'des Roses'. True, there was a garden attached to the house, which in itself is quite a rarity in Paris, but since Monsieur and Madame Brulot had moved in – more than sixteen years previously – no one had lifted so much as a finger towards its upkeep, so that all roses and other flowers were things of the past. Moreover, it got very little sun, as the neighbouring houses cast their giant shadows over the whole plot. The only thing able to survive such conditions was the grass, thriving as it does all the more the less it is cared for, and delighting in neglected masonry and incipient ruins.

Making the best of a bad job, Madame Brulot had soon decided to keep chickens, and about thirty of them now scratched about in the 'grounds' of the Villa. And as though Paris did not exist and the sun never set on their empire, the creatures actually laid eggs, which were sold in town by Madame at twenty centimes apiece. For her garrison she bought Italian eggs at half the price, and secreted them about the garden early in the morning, after which they were carried triumphantly into the kitchen. Though there might be the occasional complaint about the meat dishes or the coffee, on the subject of the eggs the ladies and gentlemen were all agreed: they were quite simply without equal anywhere in town.

Affixed to the wall next to the front door was a black notice-board, which carried the following announcement in gilt lettering:

VILLA DES ROSES
MAISON C. A. BRULOT

PENSION DE FAMILLE DE PREMIER ORDRE
TOUT LE CONFORT MODERNE GRAND PARC POUR ENFANTS

PRIX DIVERS ET À CONVENIR

DÉJEUNERS ET DINERS AU CACHET

ENGLISH SPOKEN

'First-class family boarding-house' was something of an exaggeration. As far as 'modern conveniences' were concerned, these consisted largely of the fact that guests were immediately given a front-door key and so could come and go as they pleased at night without having to get anyone out of bed. On the other hand, the place did not run to electric lighting or a bathroom. Whenever some newcomer, starting to feel grubby after a week or so, inquired about them, Madame Brulot would explain that she had decided to forgo both newfangled inventions because of the attendant dangers. The gutting of the Bazar de la Charité department store, in which several hundred people lost their lives, had in Madame Brulot's opinion been caused by a short circuit in the electrical system, while just across the road from the Villa a bailiff of less than forty had suffocated in his bath, without the neighbours hearing so much as a cry for help.

'Lunch and dinner extra' meant that one could take meals at midday or in the evening without being a resident, so that the number of mouths to feed tended to fluctuate somewhat. 'English spoken' dated from the time when one of the paying guests was a gentleman who had lived in London and liked to show off his English. Madame Brulot still knew about five words, such as 'yes', 'no', 'money', 'room' and 'dinner'.

Let us render unto Caesar the things that are Caesar's. It should be said in Madame Brulot's favour that the food, apart from one or two minor items and the egg business, was really not all that bad. She bought the ingredients personally and the preparation was entrusted to a kitchen maid, helped by a chambermaid who usually also had some notion of cookery. The fare, at least for the two large communal meals which began at twelve noon and seven in the evening respectively, was the same for all guests. And yet the prices they paid varied considerably. Several factors were more or less decisive in determining price: firstly the size, location and furnishings of the room one occupied, the quantity of food one consumed, the financial reputation of one's country of origin (Americans, for example, were as a rule charged more than Poles or Armenians), and finally the health and age of guests as this affected the degree of nuisance they caused. Accordingly, guests were always accepted for a trial period only, be it a week or a month, according to the impression they made on Madame Brulot at the initial interview, and with the weight and cubic capacity of accompanying luggage also being taken into account. However, this last factor had become less and less decisive since Madame Brulot had had deeply distressing experiences with some outsize suitcases.

Though she had had time enough over the years to perfect her knowledge of a subject which was after all part and parcel of her trade, Madame Brulot was still often badly mistaken in her assessment of newcomers. She could not, for example, entirely rid herself of the preconceived notion that fat people usually have large appetites for food and drink and thin people small ones, without reflecting that the obese are often forced to observe moderation while skinny folk frequently have tapeworms, with of course disastrous results for any boarding-house. In addition she continued to accept the occasional defaulter, though each time she swore by God and all the saints that she would never be caught out again.

However, it was no easy task to keep mangy sheep out of an establishment whose good name one was anxious to preserve by not requiring payment in advance, for as is always the case in business the Brulots were constantly exposed to all kinds of schemes, ruses and sharp practices dreamt up by unscrupulous competitors.

One example will suffice. It so happened that Madame Durand, who ran the boarding-house Sweet Home in the same neighbourhood, had once taken in a delegation of four Serbian gentlemen dispatched to Paris by their government to make a thorough study of the latest developments in fire-fighting and the education of backward children. They were given nothing but the best, since everything was billed to the Serbian legation, the head of which was even invited to dinner so that he could be introduced to Madame Durand, who felt extremely honoured by such kind consideration. Until one day a chap from Brussels stopped off at Sweet Home and, hearing the gentlemen talking to each other, recognized the four as hailing from his home town. Great was Madame Durand's consternation, especially since it had been agreed that a month's notice should be given, meaning that the delegation was entitled to stay on for another thirty-one days. After much argument back and forth, a mutually acceptable compromise was arrived at. The gentlemen were prepared to leave Sweet Home immediately, on condition that Madame Durand gave her word of honour not to involve the police, and directed the members of the delegation to a respectable *pension* where they could resume their activities. Both conditions were strictly adhered to, and so it was that the four Serbians wound up at the Villa des Roses, where they lived for five months.

So that one is bound to admit that the forty-five-year-old Madame Brulot was faced with an onerous task, particularly in view of the fact that her husband concerned himself very little with the business and that Madame also worked as an inspector for the city's Poor Relief Committee. Her job consisted of paying visits to destitute new mothers every other day, which brought her in an additional two hundred and fifty francs a month.

Madame was careful to keep the boarding-house's accounts separate from the money she earned with the Poor Relief Committee, and whenever, as in a case like that of the Serbians, she was forced to dip into her private kitty, she never failed to ask Monsieur Brulot whether or not he now realized that she was losing her own money.

Rumour had it that Madame Brulot actually made much more than two hundred and fifty francs a month from the Committee, and was the special protégée of the head of her department. This, so it was said, was the real reason why she had already received two decorations and a diploma. The diploma hung on the wall in the 'banqueting room', and she always pinned on her decorations before setting off on her rounds.

Whatever the truth of the matter, one thing that was certain was that so-called *petits bleus* would often arrive for Madame, that is, notes which were sent all over the city by air pressure through a system of tubes and usually reached the addressee within the hour – definitely not a good sign. But of course she was old and wise enough to know what to do and what not to do.

Madame Brulot was not unpleasant in appearance, although she lacked distinction on account of the excessive fleshiness of her nose, which resembled a Bourbon nose the way backstreet mongrels are sometimes reminiscent of pedigree fox terriers. The reason was that she suffered from an ailment principally characterized by an itching and swelling of the membranes of her nose and mouth whenever she ate certain fruits or vegetables, especially strawberries and bananas, and as a result of the constant rubbing to alleviate the itching her nose had swollen and developed a number of strange folds which gave her a permanently aggrieved expression. Madame Brulot was corpulent, though not excessively so for her age; she had a heart of gold, made her own hats, and was able to make herself look quite attractive with the help of a few cheap accessories.

Monsieur C. A. Brulot was twenty years older than his wife, around sixty-five, and had, it seemed, been a village notary by profession. Madame Brulot had once borne him a son, who had died at the age of six and was buried in the village churchyard. This was one of the few events which had ever moved Monsieur Brulot deeply, but Madame Brulot particularly had wept incessantly, and for weeks on end had stood outside the cemetery gates after closing time so as to be able to watch the little bush which grew on the grave. According to Monsieur Brulot this had been the main reason why he had sold his practice and come to Paris to run the Villa des Roses. He had hoped that his wife would find more to take her out of herself in the capital, and in that respect at least his expectations were not disappointed. However, his successor had paid him only in part or had played some other dastardly trick on him, since even now, a good sixteen years later, Monsieur Brulot was said to be still involved in litigation in pursuit of his claim. To this end he was forced, three or four times a year, to call on his wife's capital, and each time she solemnly assured him that this was the last time.

Monsieur Brulot had a bald patch, fringed with long grey hair, and still wore a black skullcap, the only item he had retained from his days as a notary. He had also served in the army in the war of 1870 and been taken prisoner by the Germans,[2] which was why he still sported a fairly warlike moustache and a goatee beard. In the afternoons, after the plates and glasses had been cleared away, he could be seen sitting in the so-called banqueting room, up to his ears in the dossiers pertaining to his case, and whenever Madame Brulot appeared he would mutter, 'I'll get that scoundrel yet.' Monsieur Brulot suffered alternately from gout, head and chest colds, afflictions of the gall-bladder and liver, and diabetes, but without succumbing to any of them, and, when he was laid up in bed and Madame was away, none of the maids dared to go into his room when he called them to give him his medicines. Consequently they had not the least respect for his age and did not think twice about knocking his feet with their scrubbing brushes when cleaning the banqueting room.

For years Madame had kept a tiny monkey, a marmoset, which she called *mon fils* and which brought some comfort to her childless existence. When she went for walks and the weather was not too raw, she would tuck the creature, which apart from its long tail was smaller than a clenched fist, between her dress and coat, where it blended in so well with her cheap furs that not even its head was visible.

'Chico', for that was his name, was allowed to sit at table with the grown-ups, and went into particular raptures when Madame let him eat out of her mouth. His little eyes would glisten and he would let out a sound rather like the chirp of a sparrow and at the same time reminiscent of a human giggle. Chico slept between Madame and Monsieur Brulot and was jealous of all the gentlemen at the Villa except for the old notary. Madame was utterly devoted to him; when she was once faced with the choice between Chico and a very respectable English couple who paid very well but preferred not to share the table with him, she had not hesitated to sacrifice her English guests for the monkey. And Chico fully reciprocated his mistress's affection. When it was too cold for her to take him with her, he would greet her return with shrieks and strange gestures, but sometimes he had fits of stubbornness and refused to take food from her.

II

Madame Gendron

For a long time the ninety-two-year-old Madame Gendron had been the financial mainstay of the Villa des Roses. While the minimum charge for bed and board at Madame Brulot's was as low as five francs a day, the lady in question paid eighteen francs, not including the countless extra items of expense incurred by her stay at the Villa. She too had known cheaper days, when she had been ten or so years younger and could still wash herself unaided, but Madame Brulot had regularly increased her monthly board as the old lady got more and more doddery until it had reached the above-mentioned figure. The rate of twenty-five francs a day would only apply after she had, God willing, reached her hundredth birthday.

Madame Gendron was reputed to be rich, but estimates of the size of her fortune tended to vary widely. Pessimists talked of a mere five hundred thousand francs, optimists of three million. However, she no longer managed the money in question herself since she was no longer capable of managing even her own body. This was the responsibility of Monsieur Garousse, a Paris businessman who acted as intermediary between Madame Gendron and her son, a doctor in Dunkerque. For some reason or other it was impossible for Dr Gendron to have his mother at home with him. And anyway, he assured them, Mama was particularly fond of Paris, although her opinion was never sought. Well, perhaps the old dear would have agreed that she loved the capital, just as she loved everything that was asked of her.

To begin with, at Dr Gendron's insistence, Monsieur Garousse had made the occasional critical comment on Madame Brulot's monthly accounts, and a few years previously Grandma Gendron had even been temporarily removed to another boarding-house, simply to give Madame Brulot a rap over the knuckles. But the old girl had soon been brought back, as the financial outcome had been no improvement. Nevertheless the admonition implicit in the temporary removal of the doyenne of her boarders had created a certain resentment in Madame Brulot, and as she now realized that the old girl could not be put up anywhere else more cheaply than at the Villa des Roses, she never failed, whenever things were not going too well with the Poor Relief Committee, to ask Madame Gendron sarcastically 'if she wasn't by any chance thinking of running off again'.

At first glance Madame Gendron looked like a well-kept elderly lady, but on closer inspection she was clearly a very, very old woman. She was tall and carried herself frightfully straight, being quite simply too stiff to grow crooked at this point in her life. There was not much meat left on her, and her hands trembled so badly that sometimes, when she tried to put a piece of bread in her mouth, it wound up somewhere near one of her ears. She could still get downstairs by herself when the bell went for dinner, as long as she had a firm hold on the banisters. Monsieur Brulot would sometimes lend her a hand, though, and even take her into the banqueting room on his arm and show her to her place at the communal table. 'One must be gallant with the ladies,' he would say on these occasions. It was particularly when she spoke that one had the impression of extreme old age. Her voice was not hoarse; she seemed rather to have rediscovered the intonation with which she must have recited her history lessons as a child. She spoke in a monotone, sometimes losing the thread, and used phrases from a bygone age. She walked cautiously, as though she did not really trust the ground under her feet, and she would certainly have upset or alarmed the other guests with her sudden appearances, if she had not announced her approach with a continuous faint cough, like plague victims once did with the bell they had to ring whenever they ventured into the street.

The tariff of eighteen francs included a daily wash, comb and general grooming for Madame Gendron. This was taken care of by the maids, who made a game of it and had reduced the washing to twice a week. There was an army of bedbugs in Madame Gendron's room, which strangely enough did not spread through the rest of the Villa.

Every Saturday there was an assault on the vermin, but it was a hopeless battle, which none the less was not abandoned as the containment of the infestation was attributed to the weekly slaughter. However, this was a misconception for, when the old girl had been temporarily moved to another room, the whole swarm had moved with her.

After lunch Madame Gendron would get up from table a little before the others, even if it meant leaving her coffee untouched, so as to be able to pay a visit to all the other rooms on her floor. She removed something from each room, even if it was nothing more than a newspaper or an ashtray, and hid everything carefully in the empty suitcase which had stood for years like a waiting coffin in her room. Two or three times a week the contents would be emptied out by the maids and returned to their rightful owners.

It was always a painful moment for Madame Gendron. She would curse at the maids, calling them 'sluts', but the following day would start all over again, never losing heart. The other guests did not interfere with her and pretended to be taken in. And the old girl would smirk gleefully whenever some gentleman asked whether she had seen his clothes-brush, or some other object which had vanished without trace.

For that matter the poor old dear was very fond of gentlemen and was full of childish delight whenever one of them served her at table, to amuse the rest of the company. If one of them were walking upstairs ahead of her she would call after him, and if she found a newcomer upstairs alone for the first time she would call him 'darling' and try to grab hold of him.

She still liked making up, for there was an eau-de-Cologne bottle and a powder box on her washstand which she never forgot to use before leaving her room. However, since her sense of smell had deteriorated badly, the bottle was filled with water and the box with potato-flour on Madame Brulot's orders.

Occasionally Monsieur Brulot would declare his love for her in public, a joke which was invariably well received. But the old girl would have nothing to do with him, even though she was not generally very fussy, as she was afraid of the notary and did not trust him. She had seen him working on his court case a few times and had got the idea that he was preparing her will.

Twice each year, at Easter and on All Saints' Day, Madame Brulot was supposed to buy her a new dress, for which she received a hundred francs from Monsieur Garousse and was told to invoice him for a hundred and fifty. Madame Brulot, who could sew a little, would buy the material and make the dress herself as best she could. She always chose black, which doesn't show the dirt – lightweight material for summer and heavyweight for winter. The maids helped with the fitting, which took place in the banqueting room, and cheered Madame Gendron up by telling her that once the new dress was ready the man of her dreams would soon appear, while Madame Brulot, with a mouth full of pins, fitted the material around her old limbs.

Monsieur Garousse had told Madame Brulot that 'without being extravagant Madame Gendron should be given the occasional outing'. Madame Brulot understood him perfectly. Every summer she took the old lady for two drives, and put in a bill for fifty-two trips, of which Monsieur Garousse paid for twelve. Not that they were very pleasant drives, since Madame Gendron would be casting angry glances at the coachman the whole time and complaining that other people were making free with her money.

At irregular intervals, usually every six or seven months or so, her son would come to Paris to attend to a few affairs. While he was there he would do some shopping for his wife and take the opportunity of visiting his mother. He would ask Madame Brulot 'if everything was in order' and would give Mama two kisses, one when he arrived and one when he left. He would inquire in passing after the state of her health, and invariably thought she was looking well. Sometimes he would stay for a whole hour, but never missed his train home.

Madame Gendron was too old to take breakfast any more. She would stay in bed until it was time for lunch. At about half past one she would retire upstairs, make her daily tour of her floor and then return to her room, where she was left until the bell went for dinner, which began at seven and finished at about half past eight. Then she was helped into bed, where she stayed until the following lunchtime.

This was precisely why she had lived to such a great age, there being nothing better for the health than a regular routine.

III

The Other Guests

After Madame Gendron, Madame Dumoulin was the oldest guest. She was a small, thin widow of about fifty, who paid eight francs a day. Her room was the largest in the whole Villa and her bed was made of oak. She was interested in current politics because her husband, during his lifetime, had been attached to the French embassy in Tehran. She had originally hesitated for a considerable time about accepting his proposal, but had finally given way. She still remembered the Persian capital, where she had lived for several years, as a terribly hot place, which had once had a revolt involving rifles and suchlike. Moreover her husband had soon started deceiving her and afterwards things had never, ever, been the same again. Oh yes, the strangest things happen in those diplomatic circles, and one was not even free to tell the whole story. No one knew exactly what had happened, but she had certainly got the better of her husband and now had a sizeable pension. Of the three francs per day that she paid above the minimum, one at most could be on account of the superior-quality room, so that it must be assumed that she was served special delicacies at breakfast, which she took in her room every day. Every morning and afternoon, never varying her departure by so much as a minute, she would set off to spend a couple of hours in the Bibliothèque Nationale, where she got on with her embroidery, surrounded by millions of library books from all ages and peoples. Now and again she would read a little of some magazine or other, which enabled her to bring up a new subject at table almost every day. She usually discussed historical questions or else exhumed dead poets and other great men. After the usual hellos and a word or two about the weather or the soup, she would, for example, maintain 'that that Madame de Pompadour,[3] Louis

XV's mistress, was really an odd woman', or 'that she would never have believed such a thing of the poet Lamartine.'[4] Monsieur Brulot, who realized that he must do his bit for the good of the business, would then reply in a forthcoming manner, 'What was that you said?', and Madame Dumoulin would launch into a 'Can you imagine . . .?' There would ensue a more or less animated conversation depending on the circumstances, which switched from one topic to another as the meal progressed. Madame Dumoulin would then sit embroidering till ten o'clock, for she was very good at it. She paid very promptly.

One other guest paid above the minimum, a Norwegian called Aasgaard, a thirty-year-old lawyer from Christiania, who had come to Paris for a year to learn French.

Mr Aasgaard had blond hair, a blond moustache and blue eyes, all pretty unexceptional for a Norwegian. He was strong-limbed and well educated, a very kind and warm-hearted man. Whenever his rent was due, he would get up an hour earlier so as not to be late with his payment. Before saying anything he would start blushing deeply, and whenever he was addressed he was so moved that he would shake his head at the same time as saying yes. Monsieur Colbert, a joker who only came to the Villa for dinner, taught him the rudest words for the most innocuous things, which Aasgaard noted down assiduously and later copied out neatly in his room. He was the incarnation of Scandinavia, and, whenever he came in with his clear gaze and childlike smile, a wind from the fiords blew through the stuffy dining-room, bringing down the temperature.

Next to the Norwegian sat Monsieur Martin, a businessman from Nantes, forty-eight-years-old with curly hair and gold-rimmed spectacles – not a pince-nez, but a proper pair of spectacles which fastened behind his ears like German professors wear in funny pictures. He was either a widower or divorced. About a year previously he had spent a couple of weeks at the Villa des Roses and had made an excellent impression on all the ladies and gentlemen, as well as on Madame Brulot. He had subsequently left, but six months later had returned for good, though he was no longer alone. This time he had brought with him a plump Polish lady of about fifty and also the latter's mother. After the joy of reunion had abated somewhat, he had paid three months in advance, not only for himself but also for the two ladies, a total of fourteen francs per day, as Madame Brulot charged only nine francs for both mother and daughter. He had had a quiet word in advance with Madame Brulot, and she, with a sidelong glance at the Polish daughter, had replied, 'Yes, of course. No, it doesn't matter at all.'

'You'll see that they're both very nice,' Monsieur Martin had said, whereupon the three of them had moved into one large room with two beds. They had now been at the Villa for seven months, but since those first bountiful months had paid nothing more, which was of course a nuisance, both for them and for Madame Brulot. It was not so bad for the mother, but Martin and the daughter were in a very awkward situation. After all, he was the person legally responsible, having brought the other two with him, and she was probably the cause of it all. During the fourth and fifth months Martin had managed to make himself useful by providing some of his business expertise to Monsieur Brulot; however, from the sixth month onwards the atmosphere was too grim for him to go on doing this. Monsieur Martin rarely contributed to the conversation at table; now and then he would wipe the sweat from his brow and try as far as possible to avoid Monsieur Brulot's gaze, which carried the constant message 'I know your game, my lad.' The Polish daughter, whose name was Marie and who was addressed as Madame Martin, also clearly felt the uneasiness of this transitional period. If Madame Brulot had known for certain that there was really no chance of further payment, the worst would have been over and the situation clear. But as things stood it was depressing. And yet with the best will in the world she could not possibly jump the gun and tell Madame Brulot how things were, since Madame was bound to realize this for herself. Meanwhile it pained her to see Madame Brulot's countenance alternately expressing hope and despair, while the resignation of someone faced with a *fait accompli* was entirely absent. Yes, the Polish woman was at bottom a very kind-hearted soul, and would gladly have put Madame Brulot out of her misery. She had even considered changing boarding-houses so as not to make things worse, but Monsieur Martin would not hear of it, since that would mean having even more people on their backs, not to mention the inconvenience of moving. The mother adopted a neutral position, taking refuge behind her scant knowledge of French and acting as though she were suffering from constant toothache, hoping in this way, mindful of the approaching nemesis, to elicit sympathy. And saintlike, Madame Brulot went on adding every sandwich and every bar of soap to the irredeemable bill.

The room next to Monsieur Martin's was occupied by three young ladies from Budapest, sisters with unpronounceable names. They were pretty girls, especially the youngest, who was tall and pale-complexioned and always wore a red ribbon in her black hair, her centre parting running back in a white line from her forehead. They went out walking every day, received lots of mail and ate more chocolate than meat and bread. They were irregular payers, at times a day early and at others a week late, but they did pay, and in the most varied assortment of currencies; mostly, though, with American notes or English pounds.

Next to Madame Dumoulin at table sat Mr Knidelius, a diminutive chap who looked about sixty but may have been younger or older. This personage was a Dutchman by birth and had spent thirty years without a break on Java. But now, in his declining years, he had probably had the urge to take a last look at his homeland before laying him down to rest amid his paddy-fields with his face turned to the scorching tropical sun. He had disembarked at a Mediterranean port as he wanted to take the opportunity of seeing the Eiffel Tower and Napoleon's tomb. And so he had now been staying at the Villa for three whole months, without showing the slightest desire to cover the remaining four hundred kilometres that separated him from the land of his birth. This, together with other oddities in Mr Knidelius's behaviour, led to the ladies' being somewhat apprehensive of him. For example, he had once hurt his finger and bled profusely, but had gone on lacing up his boots without even thinking of first stanching the flow of blood, and had afterwards simply stuck his finger in his mouth. And even though he always wore slippers and spoke in a high-pitched voice, you could tell at a glance that Mr Knidelius had been long resident in a country crawling with huge spiders, where at night one could hear the sounds of tigers conferring with one another in the moonlight. He had a large number of Christian names, as his letters were addressed to 'J. A. D. Knidelius Czn, Esq.'. The kitchen maid was particularly intrigued by the 'Czn' bit.[5] Madame Brulot was under the mistaken impression that he was a little deaf, and always spoke to him in a loud voice or with accompanying gestures, even though his hearing was as keen as a poacher's.

Also staying at the Villa was a girl who claimed to come from Brittany and to earn her living by giving music lessons. Her name was Jeanne de Kerros. She had arrived at night, so that all that could be seen was that she had a limp, but no one had noticed anything special about her. However, the next day, in the light, she turned out to have white blotches on her neck and the back of her head was rather like the skin of a coconut, because the hair had grown in such a peculiar way and looked as though it could be ground to dust like saffron between one's fingers. She also always took pills before meals, and the upshot was that no one wanted to sit next to her at table. At her wits' end, Madame Brulot put her between Aasgaard, who would not dare complain, and an empty chair, which nevertheless had a place laid in front of it, designed to give the impression for the first few days that someone else was expected. After that she would get used to it. Putting her between *two* empty chairs was simply unthinkable.

The twelfth and last full boarder was a young German called Grünewald, who worked in an office somewhere and had rather bad manners. For example, he would start whistling at table if one dish did not follow the other quickly enough. He also cut up his meat before starting on his meal so he could eat it non-stop, and drank a lot of wine, white and red indiscriminately.

It should be mentioned that wine was not charged separately and that everyone could consume as much as they liked. Madame Brulot served it from barrels, one of red and one of white, which lay side by side in the cellar. It cost her no more than fifty centimes a litre. Whenever she informed prospective guests about the price charged for wine in her establishment, she never forgot to add '*vin à discrétion*'.[6] Monsieur Brulot, however, maintained that large quantities of white wine were bad for the nerves, and that excessive consumption of red was just as dangerous. 'The red isn't much better,' as he put it. He himself drank wine diluted in two parts of water, and the guests followed his example, partly from false modesty and partly because they were actually a little superstitious. Only Grünewald drank his wine without water, a litre at lunch and a litre at supper, and what's more seemed to have nerves of steel. The old notary frequently tried to influence him with sarcasm.

'Please pass the wine to Monsieur Grünewald,' Brulot would say, when there were already a couple of bottles within reach of the German. At the beginning Grünewald had occasionally been in two minds, and one could see there was an inward struggle between good manners and a taste for wine, with the latter, however, invariably gaining the upper hand. But by now he seemed to have overcome his scruples once and for all. The odd thing was that Madame did not seem to mind that much. Anyway, he continued to pay a mere five francs a day, without giving it so much as a second thought.

Apart from Monsieur Colbert, the joker who made such wicked fun of the Norwegian and only dined at the Villa, there was a tall pale man named Brizard, who came for lunch and dinner. He was a nice enough sort but was subject to depression. An architect by profession, he worked all day long in artificial light, and described how his boss called him a nitwit and young lout, even though he wore a long black beard. He may also have been in love, which may have accounted for his depression, or maybe he would rather have been living with his mother in the Vosges mountains, where he came from. He still lodged opposite the station he had arrived at when he first came to Paris years ago, and one could make his day just by walking back home with him. On the way he would talk about the area where he was born and ask people if they knew it. And since everyone said that they did not, he never failed to recommend his companion to visit Moyenmoutiers, which he described as the most beautiful village in the world.

IV

The Kitchen

The food for all these people was of course prepared in the kitchen, which was on the ground floor at the front of the house and looked out on to the street through a window which was always open, in front of which the maids gathered to listen whenever a street singer passed by, and through which parcels were taken in and beggars given scraps. Three of the latter had been officially recognized by Madame Brulot, which meant that they had to be given whatever leftovers could not be used for the following day. But there were also 'outsiders', or irregular beggars, who only called in when they were in the area on other business. None of them was ever sent away empty-handed and, if all the food had been distributed, the girls would draw straws to see which of the two would give them a few sous. The winner was glad, and the loser comforted herself with the thought that those who were unlucky at games of chance were lucky in love.

Every evening, after the dinner things had been cleared away, the maids were allowed to go out, and did not have to be back at their post till seven o'clock the next morning to start preparing breakfast, so that they both had ample time to conduct their private affairs outside the Villa. Where and how they spent the night was their own business. And the fact that they had rooms in the Villa made no difference to this freedom. The reasoning behind this was that they were both given a place to sleep in part-payment, and that it was up to them whether they made use of it or not. In that respect, therefore, conditions were more democratic and there was greater personal freedom than in our more northerly climes.

Madame Brulot had had quite a bit of trouble with chambermaids recently, but she was on good terms with Aline, the young kitchen maid. She never left on Poor Relief Committee business without first dropping by the kitchen and asking Aline about her appearance. She would slowly revolve, while Aline looked her up and down with an expert eye which did not miss a thing: her heels, the pleats of her dress, her hat, her hair or her powder. With a gentle smoothing motion and a word or two Aline would correct the odd detail, after which Madame Brulot would glance in the mirror with her face close to the glass. She would wrinkle her nose, raise and lower her eyebrows, and say she was getting old and lined, to which Aline would reply that it was not at all noticeable. Madame would adjust her veil, pick up her bag, lift the hem of her dress a little way off the ground, revealing a glimpse of white lace, and step determinedly out into the world, carefully avoiding the puddles when crossing the street. 'Old bag,' said Aline, watching her through the window.

All letters were also delivered to the kitchen. Letters arrived for Mr Knidelius with the correct address in full on which there was never any postage due; the young Hungarian ladies received blue- and pink-coloured letters, Martin registered ones and Madame Gendron no letters at all. The morning post was brought to every- one in bed with their breakfast by the chambermaid, and anyone expecting news during the day would drop in to the kitchen to ask if there was anything for them. Anyone wanting to get their mail promptly had to be sure to tip the maids at the end of the month, and most of the guests did so. Only Madame Dumoulin and Madame Gendron never gave anything, the former on principle, the latter for a threefold reason: she was too mean; as has already been mentioned she received no letters; and finally she never knew when one month was over and the next had begun. She had lost all sense of time and, up in her room, above the large suitcase, there hung a forgotten calendar from the year when Madame Gendron had been welcomed to the Villa as a new guest.

V

Louise

A new chambermaid had arrived whose name was Louise and who dressed in black. She never missed a day in washing Madame Gendron, and her coming to work there was bad news for the bedbugs. She did not make much fuss, but it was clear from the sound of her voice that she took things seriously.

VI

Cherchez la femme

As happened with every new maid, all the gentlemen at the boarding-house, with the exception of the Norwegian, had descended on Louise like a swarm of flies round a jam jar. And since they were all differently inclined, each had employed his own method.

Monsieur Brulot, who was already well over sixty and realized that impetuousness no longer accorded with his years, had gone for the fatherly approach. He stayed in bed for half a day and, once Madame Brulot had gone off to the Poor Relief Committee, he had called for Louise to come and give him his medicine. He had given her an affectionate pat on the head and said that she had the makings of a capable nurse, adding that those dark eyes of hers were devilishly attractive. But when he had tried to get her to put a compress on his stomach, she had left, abandoning him to his fate.

Monsieur Martin, who in his room was hampered by the constant presence of the two Polish women, had spoken to her in the banqueting room while she was laying the table and asked her, without looking up from his paper, when and where 'a meeting could be arranged' to discuss some very important matters in private. Louise had not answered and when Madame Dumoulin came in at that very moment Martin had said, quite unperturbed, 'That's all right, Louise, I'll sit in my usual place. Don't you worry.'

Mr J. A. D. Knidelius Czn had put his faith in the power of money and, like Monsieur Brulot, had chosen his bed as the best location. So, one morning when she brought him breakfast, she had found a five-franc piece on his bedside table. To prevent the cup from wobbling, she had picked up the coin and put it on the tray. Mr Knidelius had pretended to be asleep, but when she made to leave the room he had suddenly opened his eyes and brought his scrawny arms, a relic of his time in the colonies, out from under the blankets. In his hand he held a reserve five-franc piece, which he put beside the first on the tray, while at the same time he had moved over to make room for her, and had smiled wanly and expectantly in her direction. Louise had left, shaking her head. 'Poor man,' she thought. She could not hold it against him, since he had behaved much better than most gentlemen usually did. And she remembered her previous job, where an old sea captain had lain in wait for her behind the door, and then charged resolutely at her on all fours. The following morning she took Knidelius his breakfast in bed as though nothing had happened, and when the end of the month came round she did not even refuse to accept the usual tip from him, which on this occasion he had doubled and offered to her without daring to look her in the face.

After Brulot, Martin and Knidelius it was the turn of Grünewald, who had no girlfriend and was bored with being on his own. The German had the double advantage over the three old men of being young and good-looking, and of proceeding much more discreetly, as he was far less experienced. After dinner he often came for a chat in the kitchen, and Aline, who quite liked him because despite everything he went on drinking lots of wine, would pour a couple more glasses and tell him what she thought about the goings-on of Madame Brulot and all the other guests. They would discuss what chance there was of Monsieur Martin's coughing up, how much the management of the Villa actually made each month out of Madame Gendron, what affliction Mademoiselle de Kerros was really suffering from, and how Madame Brulot had come by her diplomas. Louise did not take much part in these conversations, but whenever Aline got on to the new-laid eggs or Monsieur Brulot and the Poor Relief Committee, she would join in the mirth with a bright laugh which never became a guffaw.

One spring evening when the weather was particularly mild and the dinner things had been cleared away ahead of time, Aline had to go into town to try on a new dress. She asked Louise to go with her, and she did not like to refuse, being an obliging sort. Whereupon Grünewald asked if he might accompany the two ladies. The wine had put him in a cheerful mood and he absolutely insisted on making it his treat. So off they went together, with Grünewald between the two girls, but without linking arms, as Aline did not want to for fear of running into her boyfriend, while Louise refused politely but firmly without entering into any further discussion.

Things took quite a time at the seamstress's, and meanwhile Grünewald walked up and down the street with Louise. And each time they turned round he cast a sideways glance at her.

'What on earth is keeping Aline?' asked Louise at last.

'Must still be with the seamstress,' said Grünewald. 'How are you liking it at the Villa? Don't you feel a bit lonely?'

'She might get a move on.'

'Yes, but you know what it's like trying on a dress. I don't know anybody here in Paris except one or two people at the German Club and *they're* beginning to bore me.'

'I could go in and ask if she's nearly ready.'

'I wouldn't bother, she'll be back shortly anyway. People don't seem to care much for Germans around here generally. I'd really like to get to know a nice girl, though.'

'It's not all that difficult,' said Louise, laughing. 'Why don't you try talking to one of those three young Hungarian ladies? Take your pick.'

'No,' said Grünewald, 'they're not my type. All that foreign currency. Better not ask how they come by it. But what about you, Mademoiselle Louise, do you already have a boyfriend?'

'My little boy takes up all my time, Monsieur Grünewald.'

'Little boy? Have you got children then?'

Louise blushed, because her motherhood gave him the chance to strike an intimate tone.

'Just the one,' she said. 'He'll be seven on 1st May. My husband's birthday was 30th April. There was only one day's difference. He doesn't live with my parents in Chevreuse, but in Rambouillet[7] with an uncle, a brother of my mother's, who hasn't any children of his own. And he's sending him to a good school. Last year he was top of the class, but it won't be so easy this year, because a new boy's arrived who's apparently very clever.'

'So you're a widow then?'

'For more than four years, Monsieur. He died on Ascension Day.'

Just then the door slammed and Aline came towards them. She immediately began giving a technical description of her new dress, which she interrupted to remind Grünewald of his promise to buy them a drink. So they went into a café, where Grünewald had a large glass of wine, Aline a small triple sec, the most expensive item on the list, and Louise did not want anything as she was not thirsty. Aline said she was being a killjoy, since you did not have to be thirsty to have a drop of liqueur. So Louise also had a glass of triple sec, but did not finish it, since she found she did not like the taste. Whereupon Aline downed it, putting her own, empty glass down in front of Louise while she did so. 'Go on, down the hatch,' said the German, who had pinned all his hopes on buying them drinks. Afterwards they walked back to the Villa and went to bed. Grünewald gave the girls a despairing look as they said good night. He did not think it was fair that he should have to go to bed alone after they had made him pay for those triple secs.

VII

Brizard and Madame Gendron

It was Saturday afternoon and raining. Madame Brulot was getting ready to go out and her husband was sitting in the dining-room leafing through his dossiers. In Martin's room there was an argument going on in Polish, in muffled tones as it was so quiet in the Villa.

Suddenly Monsieur Brizard came in. He shook off the raindrops and put his head round the kitchen door to say hello to the maids.

'How's my dear Monsieur Brizard, and how's his love life?' asked Aline, brushing a lock of hair off her forehead with the back of her hand.

Brizard smiled.

'I'm very well, thanks, Aline, but I'm afraid it won't last much longer.'

'I don't think that man's very happy,' observed Louise.

'Looks pretty gloomy anyway,' said Aline. 'Just look at this disgraceful piece of sirloin,' she went on, putting the evening's joint away in the cupboard with a contemptuous shove.

'*Bonjour!*' called out Madame Brulot from her room, recognizing Brizard's voice.

Brizard went into the drawing-room for a moment, took off his hat and coat and then walked into the garden.

Bang! There was a dull report, followed by furious squawking and flapping of wings from the chickens, which were shut up in the chicken-run because of the bad weather.

Madame Brulot had such a fright that she almost dropped her powder-case, and came rushing into the kitchen, pale and completely distraught.

Monsieur Brulot took off his pince-nez and looked up with a puzzled expression, while in Martin's room, where they were obviously afraid that this was the beginning of the end, the door was locked from the inside.

What was it? No one dared to go and look.

'I want to know what happened,' announced Monsieur Brulot and went to look upstairs, although everyone had clearly heard that the noise had come from the garden.

Meanwhile there was no second report, so that Madame Brulot finally summoned the courage to go over to the French windows and look outside. She saw something lying near the chicken-run that did not belong in the garden. Could it be Brizard? It could scarcely be anyone else. From upstairs Monsieur Brulot was heard to say 'Damnation!', presumably because he had not found anything. Madame Brulot rushed to the foot of the stairs and screamed, 'Casimir, Casimir, come quickly, it's Brizard, he seems to have shot himself in the head.' She called her husband by his Christian name for the first time in three years. Casimir came downstairs and inquired if they had gone mad. 'Can't you hear what I'm telling you?' said Madame Brulot, pushing her husband into the garden, followed by Aline and the Polish daughter, who had meanwhile realized that this had nothing to do with outstanding bills.

Brizard was lying on his side. He had fallen on the grass, so that he was wet but not muddy.

'Clown,' said Monsieur Brulot as he bent over him, as he did not want to be taken for a fool and still had a faint hope that it might be just a joke, especially as Brizard was pulling a face as though he were trying hard not to laugh. But it was not a joke, because they now saw that there was blood trickling from his mouth.

'Come on,' Brulot ordered the three ladies, 'help me carry him inside.' And to Louise, who was standing in the French windows, he said, 'Go and fetch a doctor.'

Monsieur and Madame Brulot grabbed a leg each, Aline and the Polish daughter an arm each, all five of them white as sheets. Halfway, Brizard was set down for a moment as the Polish woman could go no further and had let go of an arm.

'Come on, I'm telling you,' ordered Monsieur Brulot again. 'Think of the neighbours.' And sure enough, windows were opened here and there and heads peered out. Brizard was picked up again and this time they managed to get him into the dining-room.

'Put him on the old sofa,' instructed Monsieur Brulot, 'that'll be softer for him to lie on.' Chico fled under the wardrobe.

'Hold on to him for a moment.' Brulot took off his coat, rolled up his shirtsleeves, and lowered Brizard on to the sofa in such a way that he could only slump over to the right, against the wall.

Brizard remained in a sitting position unaided.

'He's not dead,' said Monsieur Brulot. 'Hortense, quick, give me some smelling-salts. This'll give your boarding-house a fine reputation,' he added bitterly, with an angry look at Madame Brulot as she came hurrying up with what he had asked for. 'Aline, go and wait at the front door, and don't let anyone in except the doctor.'

He held the bottle under Brizard's nose, while Madame Brulot loosened his collar. Suddenly Brizard moved his lips, gave a couple of frog-like puffs and then all at once collapsed like a snowman that has had boiling water poured over it. He fell to the right, and the wall broke his fall, just as Monsieur Brulot had foreseen. Madame Brulot stepped back in dismay.

The doctor appeared. He took off his gloves and asked Brulot, with a motion of his head in Brizard's direction, 'if it was for that gentleman'.

'That's right, doctor,' replied Monsieur Brulot. 'I think he's shot himself through the mouth.'

The doctor felt his pulse and listened to his heart. Finally he looked Brizard up and down and asked Monsieur Brulot if it was his son.

'No, doctor, but he's one of my guests.'

'He's dead,' said the man. 'I'll write out the certificate and send it to the police.'

The onlookers were speechless for a moment, and Marie's mother now joined the others. The doctor left and Monsieur Brulot sent Louise to the police to ask them to fetch the body before dinner if possible. 'Where shall we put him in the meantime?' Brulot asked his wife when they were alone. 'We can't possibly leave him here in the banqueting room. And what if they can't fetch him till tomorrow. You can never rely on them. And tomorrow's Sunday, so it might be Monday. A pretty kettle of fish.'

'*Mon Dieu*,' sighed Madame Brulot, 'it's awful. And I haven't got a single bed available. The poor devil owed me for eighteen dinners and eighteen lunches too. We'd best write to his parents in Moyenmoutiers for the seventy-two francs. Not right away, though.'

'You're right,' said Brulot. 'Leave it on his tab for now. We'll put him on a couple of blankets in the maids' room for the time being.'

Madame Brulot shrugged her shoulders.

'What an idea. How would Aline like that? She'd never dare sleep in the room again.'

'It isn't a case of what she likes,' said Monsieur Brulot. 'Or are we supposed to let that bitch of a kitchen maid lay down the law to us?'

'You're out of your mind, man. Do you think I'm going to upset all my staff just to please you? Do you know what we could do? Put him in Madame Gendron's room for the moment. She'll think he's asleep. They won't be taking him away before dinner, and we can decide what's to be done later this evening.'

Monsieur Brulot had not thought of that, and agreed to the suggestion.

Helped by Aline and the Polish daughter they picked Brizard up again and carried him upstairs.

Madame Gendron was sitting in a wicker armchair waiting for dinner, and when she saw the procession coming in said that surely the dinner bell had not gone yet?

'Of course it hasn't,' Madame Brulot reassured her, 'dinner won't be ready for another hour. Look, Madame Gendron, it's Monsieur Brizard. You don't mind if he has a rest on your bed till after dinner, do you?'

'Why not?' replied Madame Gendron. 'Go right ahead, Monsieur Brizard.'

'We could put a used sheet under him and a second one on top. That'll look tidier,' suggested Madame Brulot.

Aline went to fetch two sheets that had been put out ready for the laundrywoman and spread one over the bed. Brizard was laid on top of it and covered with the second sheet.

'Are you coming downstairs with us, Madame Gendron?' asked Brulot.

'No,' said the old girl, 'no thank you. I'll come down when dinner's ready.'

Brulot shot a questioning look at his wife.

'Leave her here then,' she said, 'I don't think it can do any harm. Aline, you can go back to work, otherwise you'll never get dinner ready tonight. Poor man, what a dreadful blow for his parents.'

All four of them left the room, with Aline in front followed by the Polish woman, who went back to her mother, not daring to stay alone with the Brulots for fear that the notary would bring up the subject of payment.

The old woman was left behind with the corpse. Silence descended on the room, where one heart had stopped and the other was scarcely beating.

Finally Madame Gendron rose from her chair, went over to the washstand, rubbed some potato-flour into her cheeks and approached the bed. She was trembling, as she had done on that evening long, long ago when she had been alone with a man for the first time.

'Hello,' she whispered.

As Brizard did not reply, she pulled the sheet off the corpse with cumbersome movements, so that the light, which had previously shone on the sheet, now fell on the white face and black beard. The eyes were open.

When Brizard had been brought in, she had not been able to see him clearly and the mention of his name had not registered with her, as the only names she knew were Brulot and Gendron. But now that she was standing so close to him and staring into his face, she remembered that she had met him at table.

'Aren't you the one who always has two helpings of meat?' she asked amiably.

Brizard said nothing.

'I shan't keep you waiting,' the old woman went on.

She managed to drop on to one knee without falling over, and tried to take off her slippers, which were done up with buckles for the convenience of the maids. She pushed and tugged at them in vain, but could not undo them, and the effort of bending over made the two veins in her temples bulge.

When she was convinced that all her sweating and straining was useless, she grabbed the sheet and pulled herself upright again.

'I don't know what's wrong, but I can't undo the things,' she confessed, 'would you mind helping me?'

This time it struck her how obstinate his silence was. She looked closely at his hands, which lay peacefully by his side.

'He looks funny today,' she thought, and decided to go back and sit in her chair, because she had become uneasy without knowing how or why, just as Chico sometimes became alarmed when a fly landed on the table, while on other occasions he would swallow the most gruesome insects alive with great relish.

The bed was so placed that Brizard's head was by the window through which the light was coming, while his legs were stretched out towards the dark side of the room. So when she reached her chair, which was at the foot of the bed, she was looking into the light, and suddenly caught sight of something gleaming around the dead man's midriff. Madame could not take her eyes off the bright spot, and instead of sitting down she hesitantly retraced her steps and bent over Brizard to get a better look.

It was a long gold chain which ran through a buttonhole and into two waistcoat pockets.

She tugged at it, at first very carefully, as she was not sure what was the matter with this reclining figure, who she already knew did not move a muscle, and then gave it a jerk so that the button came off. From one pocket there emerged a gold watch and from the other a silver pencil. The old woman started, and stood listening in silence for a moment. Then she pulled the chain and the pencil through the buttonhole and held the watch and its appurtenances in her hand.

As fast as her legs could carry her she went over to the large suitcase, opened it and put the booty inside.

Then she realized that it might be just as well to put the sheet back in place.

She picked it up and spread it over the body, leaving only the shoes visible.

The bell summoning the guests to dinner resounded through the Villa.

VIII

A Shared Vigil

In the drawing-room, next to Brizard's hat, Aline had found a letter addressed to Madame Brulot. Madame Brulot tore it open hesitantly, since now that he had died still owing her for those dinners she only half trusted his last will and testament. In the envelope were a sheet of paper with writing on it and a banknote, of which Madame Brulot quickly turned back the comer so as to see the figure indicating the denomination. Then she read the following letter, crumpling up the note in her hand as she did so to keep it from prying eyes:

Dear Friends,
Now that I am about to die, it is my duty to bid you all a brief but sincere farewell. Life is hell, my friends, and we, the proletariat, take the brunt of it. That is why I am ending it all, but at the same time I express the hope that your paths may be strewn with roses. For I bear no hatred towards anyone and have asked my old mother for forgiveness.

Farewell to all of you, who have sat at the same table with me so often.

And this evening, when you are once again gathered together and are sitting chatting pleasantly to each other, spare a thought for

Yours truly,
GUSTAVE BRIZARD

P.S. Madame Brulot, I still owe you seventy-two francs. I am enclosing a hundred-franc note and hope that you will accept twenty francs from me to make up for the bother I have

caused. I should like to donate the remaining eight francs in
my name to your Poor Relief Committee. I have also written
a letter to the Commissioner of Police requesting him to send
my body to Moyenmoutiers, where I was born and where I
wish to be buried. Adieu.

Tears welled up in Madame Brulot's eyes as she read 'I have asked
my old mother for forgiveness', but when she reached the point
where Brizard asked the assembled gathering to spare a thought for
him, they simply rolled down her cheeks and on to the letter.
Perhaps she was thinking of her little son, who was also buried in a
village churchyard. As she always did when something happened to
upset her composure, she called Chico, who immediately jumped
on to her shoulder and grabbed at the banknote.

'Behave yourself, you little rascal,' she scolded the monkey in a
voice heavy with emotion, 'that's from Monsieur Brizard, and you
keep your hands off it.'

She then tucked the note away for safety and went and showed
the letter to her husband.

'Let me have a look,' said Brulot earnestly. 'It's a proper will. Did
he actually enclose it?'

'Certainly,' replied Madame, tapping her pocket. 'Wasn't it good
of him to remember those few francs? It was bad enough as it was.'

'You're probably right,' admitted Brulot. 'But still it doesn't sur-
prise me completely because he was a thoroughly upright chap.
Rest assured you can't expect anything like that from Martin.
Anyway, he's too much of a coward to commit suicide.'

'You must read it out at table in a bit,' said Madame. 'It's worth
it. I couldn't bring myself to do it. Leave out the postscript, though,
because that's no one's business but ours.'

'But after I've read out the letter I'll have to pass it round anyway.
Can't you see that everyone will want a look? And what's the good
of leaving it out? That'll just make people suspicious.'

'Cut the postscript off then,' said Madame Brulot.

The notary took a pair of scissors, cut the letter in half and put
the top half of Brizard's valedictory greeting in his inside pocket.

'Don't read it straight away, mind,' said Madame finally. 'Those

Hungarian women often arrive late. Best do it after the soup, when everyone's there.'

Louise had returned with the message that the body would be collected the following morning, and shortly afterwards they had a visit from the police commissioner, who knew Monsieur and Madame Brulot personally and got the formalities over with as quickly and with as little fuss as possible. He examined the witnesses, namely the said Monsieur and Madame Brulot, Aline, Louise and the Polish woman, whose real name turned out to be Anna Krupinsky, and the various statements were taken down by a clerk. Whereupon the two of them left, taking the revolver with them.

The guests meanwhile returned to their rooms one by one, and received the news with varying degrees of consternation. The young Hungarian ladies took it hardest of all and went on discussing the matter animatedly for a long time in their strange language. As far as the Norwegian was concerned, it was impossible to explain to him in words what had actually happened. He was totally unprepared for anything like a suicide and got mixed up with the French *mort*, meaning dead, and English 'more', as he was now learning English too. Madame Brulot finally succeeded in making him understand what had happened, by raising her hand to her chin, lowering it halfway to her bosom and saying 'Monsieur'. As she did so she made the gestures of a deaf mute who is hungry and wants something to eat, and pointed to Brizard's place at the table. This was supposed to mean: 'The gentleman with the long beard who always had his meals at the Villa and sat in this place.' Then she clenched her fist, held the thumb against her right temple and shouted 'Boom!' Which meant: 'He's blown his brains out.' Finally she shook her head back and forth and made sympathetic clicking noises with her tongue. Aasgaard understood everything perfectly and asked if it had happened here in the house, whereupon Madame Brulot pointed to the garden. Then he gave voice to his feelings by saying: '*C'est très triste, il a très tort*.'[8] And he meant it, because the Norwegian meant everything he said.

As he had agreed with his wife, Monsieur Brulot rose to his feet after the soup course, cleared his throat and said the following, while Louise tiptoed about exchanging the plates much more quietly than usual:

'Ladies and gentlemen, please excuse me if I interrupt dinner for a moment. It is my sad duty to convey to you a last greeting from someone who for three years was one of the most loyal guests at table in our Villa. You are all of course already aware, ladies and gentlemen, that I am referring to Monsieur Brizard, who this afternoon, in the bloom of his youth, committed suicide in the garden of the Villa by shooting himself through the mouth. The body, ladies and gentlemen, is resting for the moment in Madame Gendron's room (Madame Gendron leant forward at the mention of her name) and will be collected tomorrow morning, barring unforeseen circumstances. Monsieur Brizard, who was a friend to you all, was thinking of you in the last moments before his death, as you will see from the following letter which he left behind. "Now that I am about to die, it is my duty to bid you all a brief but sincere farewell. Life is hell, my friends, and we, the proletariat, take the brunt of it. That is why I am ending it all, but at the same time I express the hope that your paths may be strewn with roses. For I bear no hatred towards anyone and have asked my old mother for forgiveness. Farewell to all of you, who have sat at the same table with me so often. And this evening, when you are once again gathered together and are sitting chatting pleasantly to each other, spare a thought for yours truly Gustave Brizard." That is all.'

There was a moment's silence. Monsieur Brulot sat down and Louise, who had been standing most respectfully by the door, now served up the next course. They were all deeply moved, even those who only understood half of what had been said, because they now knew that Brizard was dead, and it was very obvious that a funeral oration had been spoken. Mademoiselle de Kerros wiped away a tear and glanced sideways at the Norwegian, as if to say 'Don't you ever do anything like that.'

The first to speak was Madame Dumoulin. She observed that 'it was amazing how the number of suicides was constantly on the increase, especially in the big cities'.

'Yes,' said the Polish daughter, who realized that she was permitted to speak because the solemnity of the moment made

everyone forget old feuds, 'it is amazing, as you so rightly say.'
Madame Dumoulin was highly thought of, and it could do no harm
to stay on her good side. 'And yet suicide is as old as the world,' the
Polish woman added hesitantly.

'Indeed,' agreed Madame Dumoulin, 'you only need look at history. It began back in the earliest times. Take Socrates, for example,
who poisoned himself.'

'But that wasn't suicide in the literal sense of the word,' Colbert,
who happened to remember the story, corrected her. 'Unless I am
mistaken he had been condemned to death. But there were probably mitigating circumstances and so he was allowed to carry out the
sentence himself.'

'What a card that Colbert is,' laughed Monsieur Brulot, mashing
a potato for Madame Gendron, 'don't let him pull your leg,
Madame.'

'Have no fear,' said Madame Dumoulin, 'I know my friend
Colbert. As if it doesn't amount to the same thing. He drank the
poisoned goblet, and so he really did commit suicide. For that
matter, what about that Roman who cut his wrists in the bath and
calmly let himself bleed to death? I suppose you'll be telling me next
that that wasn't suicide either, Monsieur Colbert?' she asked sarcastically.

'Well, I won't deny that that was suicide.'

'So what are you going on about Socrates for then!'

The whole time Mademoiselle de Kerros had been anxiously
watching the Norwegian, but during the story about the man with
the dreadful veins in his wrists, she could control herself no longer
and trod on his foot, whereupon Aasgaard pushed his chair back to
see what was going on under the table. Chico, who was sitting on
his mistress's shoulder, tried to reach Madame Gendron's hair.

'It's awful,' said Madame Brulot. 'How on earth can someone
watch himself bleeding to death without calling for help? It's bar-
baric. No, for my part I'd sooner choose a revolver like poor Brizard
any time.'

'A revolver, a good revolver that is, is the quickest and the safest
way,' Monsieur Brulot assured them with all the authority of a vet-
eran of 1870.

'Revolvers make a mess,' observed one of the Hungarian ladies, 'I think I'd prefer to drown myself.'

'As if water doesn't make a mess too,' said Colbert. 'Yes, I'll have another piece, please, Louise. I once saw them fish a woman who'd drowned herself out of the Seine, and she was as swollen as anything with the water.'

'Ugh, Monsieur Colbert, will you please stop talking about such gruesome things at table,' asked Madame Brulot, 'it's enough to make a person ill.'

'All these things are equally sad,' said Madame Dumoulin, summing up. 'Just think of all the executions during the Revolution. That poor Marie Antoinette, how she must have suffered.'

'But she got what was coming to her!' ventured Monsieur Brulot, since he professed socialist principles, having so little say in the affairs of the Villa.

'So. You think so, do you?' replied Madame Dumoulin icily. 'Well, I regard it as a scandal that you men allowed such a thing to happen without lifting a finger to save your queen. And I can give you a solemn assurance that opinions like those of Monsieur Brulot would be very poorly received in diplomatic circles.'

The cheese was finished and dinner over, Madame Dumoulin took up her embroidery, the Hungarian ladies went out for a breath of fresh air, Colbert left as usual and the other guests went to their rooms, except for Grünewald, who went to the kitchen, and Madame Gendron, who stayed downstairs for the time being as either she or Brizard had to be found a bed for the night.

In the kitchen Grünewald was given a complete account of what had happened on that memorable day.

'But what are they going to do with the body?' asked Louise. 'It can't possibly stay the night in the same room with Madame Gendron.'

'Of course it can,' said Aline, 'one of them is stone dead and the other as good as, so they won't get into an argument.'

This was her way of protesting at the treatment the old woman was subjected to.

But Louise could not bear to hear her say such things.

'Stop it, Aline,' she warned, glancing at the door, 'how can you talk like that?'

'Yes, that's just nonsense,' said Grünewald, agreeing with Louise. 'But I don't mind giving up my room for one night,' he went on. 'And we can't really leave the body all alone. There really ought to be a vigil, don't you agree? At least, that's the custom where I come from. If one of you will sit up with the body till about one or two in the morning, I'll go out to a *café-chantant*[9] till then, and come and relieve whoever's on watch. It's Saturday and I don't have to go to work tomorrow anyway. Who's willing?'

'I'm too scared,' admitted Aline.

'What about you, Louise? It's right up your street.'

'I'm not scared,' said Louise, 'and I'll do it gladly. Monsieur Grünewald is quite right. We mustn't leave the man alone for that one night, even though we're not family.'

'That's settled then,' said Grünewald, seizing his chance. 'I'll relieve Louise at two o'clock. And Aline will have to make sure that coffee's ready a little earlier than usual, because as soon as it's light it'll be all right to leave him alone.'

The suggestion got Monsieur and Madame Brulot out of a difficult predicament, and the former notary clapped Grünewald on the shoulder with the approving comment, 'That's the spirit, young man!' They then fetched the Norwegian and with his help Gustave Brizard was transferred to the German's room. Louise undressed Madame Gendron, helped her into bed and tucked her up. Then she went and sat beside the body, taking pen and ink with her, as she intended to while away the time by writing a letter to her son.

A deep silence now descended on the Villa, where only Louise was still awake and doing her best not to nod off. Now and then she glanced at the dead man. He reminded her of her husband, who had also worn a beard, though not such a long one. She also thought of her village and of how she was going to spend the coming day. For it was her turn to go out, so she would be free after lunch. She also thought a couple of times about Grünewald and his decision that the dead man should not be left alone and that he would give up his bed.

At about half past one the silence was disturbed by the jingling of a carriage, followed by an argument with the coachman and the agitated tapping of a couple of walking-sticks on the paving-stones. Then the carriage drove off and the murmur of muffled conversation was heard, which went on for a while even though the key was already in the lock. Finally the sound of the walking-sticks receded down the street, the door was closed and downstairs in the hall there was the suppressed sound of girlish laughter. Then nothing more. Louise went over to the window and raised the curtain a little. She saw the two rows of lighted lampposts. There was not a soul to be seen in the whole street. On the corner was a chapel with a turret,[10] whose clock now chimed twice. It was not clear whether it was half past one or two o'clock. However, Louise was in no doubt that it must be half past one. This certainty derived from her conviction that Monsieur Grünewald would come ahead of time and was not yet there. And so it turned out, because shortly afterwards she heard hurried footsteps enter the street and stop outside the Villa. Louise, who was at the washstand freshening her face using Grünewald's towel, which she did not find at all distasteful, quickly went back to the bed and sat down by the corpse. It flashed through her mind that frivolous girls in her position would certainly pretend to be asleep. Then the door was opened gently and Grünewald came in. Louise got up.

'Well,' he asked in a whisper, 'how goes it with our dear departed?'

'Nothing special happened.'

'Haven't you had any sleep?'

'No, I've been writing a letter to Lucien. My son,' she explained, 'he lives in Rambouillet, with a brother of my mother's.' And with the tip of her tongue she licked at one corner of the envelope that would not stay closed. 'Don't you think he writes beautifully for a boy of seven? You mustn't pay any attention to that blot, that was an accident.' And she showed him the postcard, which really was very neatly written, especially the date and *Chère Maman*.

'You're telling me,' said Grünewald. 'A boy who writes like that is bound to grow up into a lawyer. But he's a bright boy. After all he was top of his class last year, wasn't he?'

'How did you know that?' asked Louise, who was not aware that she talked about her son every day.

'But it won't be easy this year,' the German went on, 'because there's a new boy, who by all accounts is very clever.'

Louise stared at him open-mouthed.

'Goodness me, I know a lot more than that. But first I want a kiss,' said Grünewald, reaching for her waist as if in childish horse-play, so that if need be he could say that he had not meant any harm. But he was pale and one corner of his mouth was curled up.

'No, none of that. Think of him,' she said, and made for the door.

'Don't get angry now, Louise, it was only a bit of fun,' Grünewald reassured her hoarsely. 'Off you go to bed, you must be very tired.' He could see that she was going anyway.

Feeling a little ashamed of himself, he whispered a silly parting remark as she was closing the door.

'The girls here are a lot different than they say in Breslau,' he thought, regretting having given up his bed.

He sat down beside Brizard and quickly fell asleep.

Only Louise lay awake for a while, thinking of everything that had happened and snuggling up to Aline, who was not even aware that someone had got into bed.

IX

The Walk

At eight o'clock the next morning, when everyone was still asleep except for Aline and Grünewald, two men arrived with a cart to take Brizard away. Aline went and knocked on the door of the Brulots' room, and from her bed Madame asked what she wanted. Aline called out that 'they'd come to fetch Monsieur Brizard', to which Madame Brulot replied that 'it was all right'. Aline led the way to Grünewald's room and the men laid the body on the large-wheeled cart. Once their cargo was safely loaded, Aline called the two of them into the kitchen and poured them both a glass of wine, which they drank straight down. The men predicted that it was going to be a nice day and left, pushing the cart ahead of them. A stranger, meeting them, would have been bound to wonder what the two of them could be selling at such an early hour, and why they were not calling out the price of their wares like most other hawkers.

At midday Brizard was still on everyone's mind, as a surprising amount of the conversation at table was devoted to him. It was felt that he had not been entirely without negative qualities. For instance, his ideas were far too radical, and he would never admit he was wrong when politics were discussed. Nevertheless, at the end of the day it was plain that such faults were outnumbered by his virtues, and he was generally agreed to have been a good sort. A lot of attention was given to the question of what could have led to his fateful decision. Madame Dumoulin was convinced that the only possible reason was disappointed love. Madame Brulot on the other hand believed that there was something else behind it, and Monsieur Brulot, catching everyone's attention with a wink, asked Madame Gendron 'what she made of it'. Louise, as she brought in the first course, cast a fleeting glance at Grünewald, as much as to say 'we two watched over him', unaware that he had gone to sleep.

Afterwards they got into long and involved arguments on the subject of executions in general, in relation to the guillotining of Marie Antoinette, which had been discussed the previous day and to which Madame Dumoulin now returned remorselessly, since she felt Monsieur Brulot had not yet made sufficient amends for his rash words. The pros and cons of the various systems in operation for carrying out the death sentence were weighed up, and most people thought that the Chinese custom of simply impaling someone on the point of a spear was the most gruesome. From Madame Dumoulin's stories, however, it was clear that the Persians should not be ruled out of contention. The American method attracted quite a lot of support as no blood was spilt. Finally they tackled the tricky moral question of whether the death penalty in France should be retained or abolished. The ladies generally favoured hard labour for life, while Monsieur Brulot thought that such scum should be got rid of every once in a while. The final conclusion was that executions were to be deplored in principle as remnants of the Dark Ages, but that in practice they proved a necessary evil. Through the windows a golden beam of sunlight fell on to the table, proving the forecast of the men with the cart correct.

After lunch Louise went out. She had decided on impulse to look up a half-forgotten girlfriend, who was a housekeeper in one of the suburbs, and whom she had known when her husband was alive. Just past the boarding-house she met Grünewald, who was standing looking at a grocer's display and asked if he might walk a little way with her. She agreed.

Louise was wearing a black dress, as always, and on her honest head was a not very elegant hat, which she could use all year round. Although the sun was shining, she had taken an umbrella and held her dress without lifting it off the ground, modestly and chastely.

Grünewald looked quite smart, but it was immediately obvious to all that he must hail from at least as far north as Lille, which coming from Paris was the southernmost tentacle of the Germanic world. Madame had tried repeatedly to teach him how to knot his tie the way it was done here, but in vain. His clothes were made of good material, but must have been sent on to him by his parents in Breslau,[11] because all his trousers looked odd, and his jackets were single-breasted with strong buttons, the sort that no one wore any longer in Paris. He certainly received occasional bulky parcels, which weighed very little and were plastered with red and yellow labels, like cases sent by rail.

Anyone seeing them walking along together, setting out like two soldiers, would have realized that those two were destined to inflict the most dreadful things on each other.

Louise's friend lived a long way away, and in the Tuileries gardens they sat down on a bench to rest for a moment. The trees were coming into leaf and boys and girls were playing and sailing toy boats on a pond.

A young man of about twenty came up, followed by a very young girl carrying a baby. It was hard to tell whether the first figure belonged with the other two, as he walked along without looking round and acted as though he had nothing to do with anybody. He seated himself on the bench where Louise and Grünewald were sitting, having ascertained at a glance that they were a couple and that there was not a single free bench. The girl sat down next to him and the baby started crying. It made a plaintive sound, in time with its mother's soothing rocking.

Louise and Grünewald looked at each other and as if by arrangement got up and continued on their way. As they left they heard the girl start speaking to the young man. An old woman stood by a tree looking at them, and Louise gave her a coin to make fate treat her more kindly and to ward off any evil.

They did not talk much. When they reached the district where her friend lived, Grünewald asked if she thought she could ever love another man, and Louise replied that she did not. Then they parted and he stood watching till she had entered the house with her umbrella.

In the course of the following week Grünewald managed to escort the girls on a couple of occasions, and, one evening as he was on his way home with Louise down an empty street, they both stopped. Grünewald said 'Louise', threw his arms round her and kissed her. Louise tried to push him away, then closed her eyes and stuttered '*mon Dieu*'.

There followed days of intense happiness for the two of them. She no longer called him Grünewald, but Richard, and in the evenings they would seek out secluded benches on which to hug and kiss. Whenever Louise served him at table, she pointed out the best morsels and, when holding out a dish to him, never failed to brush his head with her sleeve, which sent them both into raptures.

X

Perret, 25 rue Servette, Genève

Louise was a sensible girl and had already experienced enough
not to let herself be bowled over and to be able to size up the situation correctly. And so she realized, not without some dismay,
that she really was head over heels in love and that the taking of
the next step was approaching at whirlwind speed. She contem-
plated the future with alarm because she knew so little about
Richard. All she knew was that he came from Breslau and had
one brother and three sisters. What were his plans for her and
how long would the pleasure last? Louise was appalled by her
sudden weakness. To think that this was about to befall her, after
she had been faithful to her dead husband for five years and had
kissed him through her son, who was already growing into quite
a big boy, and whom she would undress completely and wash
with her own hands when she was between jobs and spending a
few days at her uncle's.

One afternoon, when she was browsing through the paper in that
half-conscious state in which, between a murder report and an advert
for pills, one revels in some old lapse or tries to anticipate the pleasure of some future sin, the following advertisement caught her eye:

PRÉSAGES. AVENIR.
Amour. Mariages. Fortune. Héritages.
ADRESSE POUR CONSULTATIONS:
PERRET, 25 RUE SERVETTE, GENÈVE.[12]

Louise flushed with surprise. This was precisely what she was looking for. That same evening, without telling anyone, she wrote Perret the following letter:

> I should like to consult you about love and what the future holds in store for me. Please write and tell me what to do and how much it costs.
>
> Yours faithfully,
LOUISE CRÉTEUR (Widow)
71 rue d'Armaillé, Paris (Aged 26)

By return of post she received the reply, which she tore open with heart pounding, and which read as follows:

> Madame Louise,
> If you require a consultation, please send two sheets of paper, each with an ink-blot. Fold the paper and rub it well, so that the ink spreads properly. I enclose a sample. Please also enclose a postal order for five francs.
>
> Yours faithfully,
PERRET
25 rue Servette, Genève

P.S. Please write your address clearly on the postal order.

The letter contained a folded sheet of paper, which when she opened it revealed a large, arbitrary but completely symmetrical ink-blot that looked like a giant butterfly. Louise got the hang of it, as she remembered from her early childhood how she used to squash flies' heads between pieces of paper, which had made similar blots, except that they had been red instead of black and of course much smaller.

She took a few sheets of paper out of one of Monsieur Brulot's dossiers and prepared two of them in accordance with Perret's instructions. However, they were not to her liking, as the blots were much too small and did not look like anything in particular.

But the question was whether she was allowed to blot any more sheets, and whether it wasn't precisely the first two which were most suitable for the consultation. Come to that, they might be the only ones that *could* be used.

On the other hand Louise was afraid that, if the sheets were no good because the blots were too characterless, Perret would ask her for a fresh pair and a second postal order as well. Louise would have been willing to use up ten postal orders for the satisfactory solution of a question so near to her heart, but if one would do, a second was unnecessary, and Louise was thrifty by nature. It also occurred to her that Perret would not suspect that she had chosen the best two from several blots and, after all, this was not forbidden by the terms of the letter.

The third and the eighth sheets seemed the most suitable to her. The blot on one reminded one immediately of a pierced heart with a crown over it, and the other also resembled something – she was sure of it – though she could not quite place the shape. It was a bit like a death's head and at the same time like a clover leaf, but wasn't really like either. Louise tore up the failures, carefully dried the two she had chosen and sent them off to Perret with the required amount.

This time the answer was longer in coming, and Louise suspected that this was because of the sheet with the strange blot on it. Perret must be racking his brains over that. But the letter finally arrived and Louise took it to Richard's room while he was at his office, in order to open it there. She locked the door, sat on the bed and began reading:

Madame Louise,
    I have received the money you sent in good order. I have studied your ink-blots and am able to tell you the following:

Dominus tecum![13]
    Your date of birth places you in the sign of Cancer. On the basis of this and of the predictions of the Great Bear and the Comets, I can tell you that two men will try to win your heart. One of them has darkish hair and the other is almost blond. One of them may have been born in Paris, the other may not. Whatever your heart tells you, do not give in to the blond one, for the dark-haired one is destined to rule your heart. With

him your fortune will be made and your happiness assured, unless Venus turns away from you. Beware of a train journey at night and of the beggar woman with the suitcase.

Should you wish to know your life expectancy and also ways of confounding your enemies, send a further three ink blots accompanied by a postal order for ten francs.

At the bottom of the letter was the initial P., but there was no sign of any other signature.

Louise was utterly dismayed. Under the sign of the Crab! Yes, she had always been fond of crabmeat and could see some connection between this predilection and her star sign. But why the Great Bear and the Comets should also be mixed up in it was a mystery to her, and the Great Bear alarmed her.

The blond man was of course Richard, who had not been born in Paris, or even in France. But what about the dark man? And then there was that awful prediction. Why hadn't it been the other way round? 'After all, he's not *that* blond,' she thought. Still, she had to admit that his hair was far from dark, however hard she tried to darken it in her mind. The dark man would win her heart. Yes, that was from the blot that looked like a heart with a crown on it. And all the rest came from that wretched sheet with the mysterious shape. She should have sent the first sheets, as she had intended to do for a moment, or the fifth one, which looked like a burning candle. But they had been torn up, and anyway it was too late. The train journey at night and the beggar woman with the suitcase made relatively little impression, because before she had read that far she was already feeling too deeply unhappy. In any case she could bear the warnings in mind. The beggar woman in the Tuileries flashed through her mind, but she had not had a suitcase with her. She did not send a new postal order, as she could no longer care less about how long she had to live and what her enemies were plotting. She was bitterly unhappy, but she could feel her love for Grünewald growing as her tears flowed.

Louise now made a last attempt to save herself, by placing her fate openly in the hands of the man she loved and begging him, if he were not sure that he wanted her to be his for as long as she chose, to leave her before she surrendered completely. She could not put it into words, not being articulate enough, and he did not seem to be able to understand from the way she looked at him, even though all that, and much more besides, was written in her eyes. So she decided to write him a letter and not to be alone with him again before she had received his reply. Otherwise he would start kissing her again and she would lose control completely. She would put the letter in his room after dinner and he would find it at night when he went to bed. She would ask for time off the next day so she could go to Rambouillet and see her son, who had written her a card asking if she were perhaps ill as for some time past she seemed to be writing much less than she used to. Her uncle must have put him up to it. That would mean that Richard would have the whole day ahead of him to take a decision, and pray God he would.

She executed her pathetic scheme just as she had planned it, and, when Grünewald came home in the evening and turned the light on in order to get undressed, he found a mauve note on his pillow in an envelope bearing the words:

MONSIEUR GRÜNEWALD
Paris.

The German, realizing at once who it was from, was pleasantly surprised. He took his penknife, slit open the envelope and took out the contents. As he unfolded the letter something fell to the ground. Picking it up, he saw it was a violet. Grünewald sniffed the flower and was delighted, even though she had chosen an artificial violet because they do not fade. He covered what she had written with his hand and read only the first and last words, which were 'Monsieur' and 'darling'. Richard put the letter, without reading it, on his bedside table, undressed and got into bed, for he had a sensual nature and did what little boys do with strawberries, saving the fattest ones till last. Then he read:

Monsieur,
    Please forgive my having taken the liberty of entering your room and delivering this letter, because I have to write and tell you what's on my mind. You say you love me and ask me to be

yours completely. But I have a presentiment that you will soon leave me, Richard, which is quite understandable. You work in a big office, know lots of foreign languages and who knows what you'll achieve one day. And how could you spend the rest of your life with a girl of my class! Perhaps after a while you will return to your homeland and then I shall be left alone, because you would not dare take me with you. After all, people in your country might say, 'Why has he brought that common woman back here?' A maid, and on top of that one who goes with you without being married. And yet you know very well, Richard, that I'm not a bad woman, the kind you pick up in the street. I loved my husband dearly and never dared think that I would be able to love another man as I love you. Besides, I have a little boy, and I would rather die than hear him say later that he had a bad mother. For that reason, Richard, I ask you not to deceive me and rather go far away without saying another word to me, if you think that sooner or later I shall have to part from you.

I shall be expecting a letter tomorrow evening, and embrace you a thousand times.

Your affectionate friend LOUISE

Tomorrow I shall be in my village all day, so there's no need to come looking for me, darling.

Grünewald was elated. He now knew that he had a sweetheart, a real sweetheart that he could do anything he liked with. It seemed to him a momentous thing to have the power to determine someone's fate, and so it was. However, the letter did trouble his conscience a little and it even occurred to him for an instant that perhaps it wasn't right to cause a lot of tears and suffering for a few moments' pleasure.

As he reflected on this he took a pencil and underlined seventeen spelling mistakes. He missed four because he did not know himself. Then he fell asleep, and in his dreams hesitation, scruples and all other such unpleasantness vanished, and what remained was an attractive young woman lying beside him with sparkling eyes, whose burning breath had the scent of violets.

Downstairs, Louise lay in her bed.

She had heard his footsteps when he came home and had heard him open the letter through all the walls in the Villa. She trembled at the thought that he might heed her plea and leave the next day, while she was at her mother's, as she was preparing lunch or with her son, who, when all was said and done, would rather be out playing with his friends.

XI

Louise's Heart

When Grünewald woke up he read the letter through again, and while he washed he sang snatches of *Trinken wir noch ein Tröpfchen*, being obliged to stop repeatedly to avoid getting soapsuds in his mouth.

On the stairs he met the Norwegian, who smiled at him by way of a 'good morning'.

Aasgaard was wearing a light blue suit and a bright red tie. He was going for a walk.

'*Spazieren?*' inquired Grünewald.

'Yes, yes,' replied the Norwegian airily. 'Want to come along?'

The Norwegian and the German had gradually become friends, which Aasgaard especially was pleased about, as with all those French people he was able to achieve very little linguistically. Besides, the other guests no longer tried to communicate with him in words, and whenever anyone, for the sake of politeness, felt obliged to consult the Norwegian on some matter or other, they simply gave him an inquiring look and Aasgaard had to decide whether this meant 'Are you conservative too?' or 'Do you also prefer asparagus to cauliflower?' Accordingly he would always answer by smiling and shaking his friendly blond head, indicating that he did not have much of a clue. Grünewald's French on the other hand, still full of German gutturals, was much more easily understood by the Norwegian, who also knew quite a bit of German.

Talking about all kinds of things, as young people do, they strolled along the river as far as Notre-Dame.

'Shall we pop in for a moment?' suggested Richard.

The Norwegian agreed.

Inside by the door was a nun kneeling on a chair and holding out a bowl, and as each coin fell jingling into it she muttered something that was lost amid the shuffling of feet under the vaulted roof. Aasgaard and Grünewald took off their hats and walked on tiptoe into the middle of the church, where they stopped. The faithful were seated in long rows and from the altar came the questioning call of the priest who moved from left to right gesturing with his arms. In the organ loft sat boys and men who answered him in song, after which the organ suddenly chimed in and drowned everything. The light in the church was dim, as though dusk were already falling.

'Come on,' said Aasgaard softly.

And leaving the praying congregation behind they made for the door.

Outside they walked on side by side without speaking, but with each of them trying to dig up something from his past which was weighty enough to merit breaking the earnest silence.

'You're not married, are you?' the Norwegian finally asked.

'No,' said Grünewald. 'I'm not married.'

'My wife,' Aasgaard went on, 'was very, very beautiful. She had long blonde hair and was a marvellous skater and pianist. I was an officer in those days and all my friends envied me. She loved me deeply, almost as much as I loved her. But, after we had been married for scarcely six months . . .'

Grünewald got the picture.

Well, what could one do about it? Why marry a wife who's so beautiful that no one can keep their hands off her?

He took Aasgaard's arm and shook him with rough sympathy. 'Come on,' he said, interrupting the Norwegian, and trying in this way to spare him a confession which must be weighing heavily on him. 'Don't let it get you down so. It can happen to the most devoted couple, and it can be patched up again.'

'No,' protested Aasgaard, 'because . . .'

'My dear fellow,' said Grünewald, defending the absent wife, 'she may have been less guilty than you think. And didn't Jesus bid the adulterous woman come unto him?'

'No,' spluttered Aasgaard desperately, 'you don't understand.

Six months after we were married, she suddenly died,' he said softly. 'Because it was so hard to forget her I came here to take my mind off it. And I'm learning French at the same time,' he concluded with a smile which began in his eyes and finished up in the corners of his mouth.

Grünewald looked for a worthy pendant to the Norwegian's intimate confidence, and thought immediately of Louise's letter, which was burning a hole in his pocket. They had sat down on a bench in the garden behind the cathedral. He gave Aasgaard a sideways glance first, but the man's whole appearance engendered such confidence that Grünewald could no longer resist and took out the letter.

'Read that,' he told the Norwegian, handing him Louise's heart. 'I got it from a woman. What would you do in my place?' He put the violet back in his coat pocket.

'There's no need for that,' said Aasgaard in embarrassment. 'I just felt like telling you.'

'No,' insisted Grünewald, 'there is a need. It's a matter of conscience and I'd value your opinion.'

Aasgaard unfolded the mauve letter with his big hands and started reading. It was quite a job for him. In the first place it was the handwriting of someone who only puts pen to paper on big occasions and in extremities, and then there were the mistakes and Grünewald's pencil-marks which made it all the more obscure. Richard had to explain to him that *j'ai un présent timen* meant *j'ai un pressentiment*,[14] and Aasgaard had to look up *pressentiment* in a pocket dictionary which he carried with him everywhere, because he did not know either it or the German word *Ahnung*. *Ramasse*, which occurred in *pourtant tu sais bien, Richard, que je ne suis pas une mauvaise femme comme on en ramasse dans la rue*,[15] was another stumbling block, as 'pick up' was being used figuratively and not literally. However, the Norwegian finally got to the end and folded the sheet with careful movements which conveyed respect.

'Well?' asked Grünewald, putting the letter away, 'what do you make of it? You won't learn any posh French from it, will you?' he said with a laugh.

Aasgaard looked at him and twiddled his melancholy blond

moustache which grew into his mouth in the middle and one end of which stood up while the other drooped hopelessly downwards.

'What are your future plans?' he asked at last.

'My plans?' said Richard. 'Well, I expect I'll help my father, who's got quite a flourishing business in oil and fat.'

'I didn't mean that,' said the Norwegian, 'I just wanted to know if you're considering marrying her.'

'Marrying? No, I shouldn't think so.'

'Then one shouldn't deceive her,' said the Norwegian, 'she's undoubtedly a good girl, my friend.'

'Yes, a lovely girl,' the German admitted, unconsciously adopting the Norwegian's solemn tone, 'but she's a widow and must have experienced a few things during her marriage. That's why I hesitated for a moment at first, but then thought that it can't really do much harm after all.'

'There are women,' said Aasgaard, contradicting him, 'who become virgins all over again when they fall in love a second time. But, my dear sir,' he added airily, as the atmosphere had become oppressive, 'you must do as you think fit; some would do it, others wouldn't.'

That remark lightened the tone and the two of them went off, as it was nearly dinnertime. People were still coming out of the church and others were pushing their way in. Among them were some English tourists, who just wanted to go up the tower.

Aasgaard and Grünewald went home, where they were awaited by Monsieur and Madame Brulot, Madame Gendron, Mr Knidelius Czn, Madame Dumoulin, the Hungarian ladies, Martin with his Polish pair, Mademoiselle de Kerros with her funny hair – in a word by the management and all the guests of the Villa des Roses, who were already seated around the communal table. Only Brizard was missing.

XII

The Wedding

While visiting her son, Louise had not been able to stand the suspense beyond about five o'clock. Towards dinnertime she reappeared at the Villa and went straight to the kitchen to ask Aline whether anything special had happened, to which Aline, without looking up from her pots and pans, replied that it had not. So he hadn't left yet. Louise went to her room for a moment to freshen up, as she was covered in dust. When she returned to the kitchen, she was wearing a white blouse for the first time since her husband had died and had put brilliantine on her jet-black hair, so that it began to gleam when she sat down at the table under the gas lamp.

Even on their days off the maids were allowed to have their meals at the Villa if they so wished. In that case they were served in the kitchen by their replacements and could imagine themselves ladies for a moment.

Louise sat with her back to the door so that he would not see her face if he came in. She was too nervous to eat properly, and nibbled absentmindedly at the carcass of a chicken which had come back from the banqueting room.

Aline gave her a cursory glance, saw the white blouse and understood everything.

'So you've made your mind up, have you, my girl?' she asked.

Louise did not answer, and picked breadcrumbs off the table. When she heard Richard's footsteps coming towards the kitchen and stopping in the doorway for a moment, she was almost sick.

'Good evening, ladies,' said the German.

'Would Monsieur like a glass of wine?' asked Aline, who was eager to do her bit to bring matters to a speedy conclusion, now she could see that everything had already been decided. She went straight over and placed a chair at the table so that he could play footsie with Louise immediately without having to execute a series of military manoeuvres first.

'*Prosit*,' said Grünewald, clinking glasses first with Aline, next with Bertha, Louise's replacement, and only then with Louise herself. All four of them drank. Louise was deeply moved. She was experiencing her wedding all over again, and Aline and Bertha realized that they were the witnesses. True, the ceremony was simpler this time, but it was still a solemn moment.

'Mademoiselle Louise,' said Richard, when the glasses had been placed back on the table, 'you look very smart. And I'd stake my life on it that I know in whose honour. You try to keep everything secret, but I've known what's going on for ages. No, you can't trust those Norwegians.'

'Well, tell me then, Monsieur,' answered Louise, without daring to look at Aline or Bertha.

'No,' said Grünewald, 'I mustn't give away secrets, even though I know you can rely completely on the silence of Aline and Bertha. And besides, I'm not absolutely certain. It's really no more than a hunch, but I'm quite sure I'm right. But I'll whisper it in your ear if you'd like me to.' Richard looked at the door to see if the coast was clear.

'Tell me, then,' said Louise invitingly, turning her head slightly towards him.

Aline went to the window and called Bertha over to her to look at something outside in the darkness.

'Half past nine on the corner by the chapel,' he whispered.

'I'm sorry, Monsieur Grünewald, but you're completely wrong,' she replied awkwardly.

When they heard her voice Aline and Bertha came back and sat at the table. Louise tried to laugh.

'So I was wrong,' said Grünewald, consoling himself.

'Alms, my little ones,' said a voice from outside, and a hand put a sack in through the window. It was Father Franciscus, the Villa's senior beggar.

'So you're back again, are you, you old rascal,' said Aline in a scolding but friendly tone, taking the sack.

'Your servant, my dear,' answered the old man, standing outside.

Aline opened a cupboard, took out various leftover items of food and put them in the sack.

'Not too many potatoes, dear child,' warned the voice of Father Franciscus.

'Are you still eating?' asked Aline, pointing at Louise's plate.

'No, I haven't any appetite this evening.'

'Pass that partridge over here then,' said Aline, putting the chicken carcass in the bag with the rest and passing the sack back through the window to its owner.

'God will reward you,' said the voice from outside, and the felt hat disappeared into the darkness.

Mademoiselle de Kerros left the banqueting room and came limping along the hall on her way to her room. One could hear her left shoe, with its raised sole, clumping on the floor through the whole house. Her white face peered through the glass door of the kitchen for a moment, because she liked at least to *see* what was going on, not being able to do anything herself.

Grünewald got up, said good evening and left. It was just striking nine o'clock.

Louise was grateful to the other two for their considerate attitude. So she put on an apron and, while Bertha went upstairs with Madame Gendron and took care of the official work, she helped Aline with the washing-up.

Just before half past nine she left the Villa. Grünewald was already waiting on the corner by the chapel. Seeing her coming, he took the letter out of his pocket and allowed himself to be caught reading it when she arrived. Louise saw him absorbed in her letter, and a smile of joy lit up her face. He gave his answer verbally as they walked arm in arm through the silent streets. It consisted mostly of 'darling', 'angel', 'eternally' and suchlike. An oath was also sworn.

At around midnight they came back to the chapel, and in a dark niche the pros and cons were weighed for the last time. Richard talked, and Louise, pressing close against him, hung on his every word. Finally, Grünewald appeared to sum up everything in a silent question which received no answer. Then they both entered the Villa des Roses and went upstairs to Richard's room. The German led the way, as is proper, and Louise followed, keeping in step with him so that Mademoiselle de Kerros, who was still awake and tossing about in her bed, thought it was only one pair of feet coming upstairs.

Grünewald locked the door, turned the light on and looked at her.

'You're very pale,' he observed, hanging his hat on the doorknob to cover the keyhole.

'Yes,' she replied.

In the middle of the night Louise came downstairs alone, in her stockinged feet and carrying her bootees in her hand. Her heart missed a beat as she passed the door of the room where Monsieur Brulot, Madame Brulot and the monkey were sound asleep and locked in each other's embrace.

XIII

Irrigation Works

Every year on the tenth of May, dinner was turned into a party by Madame Brulot, in honour of Madame Dumoulin from Tehran, whose name was Antoinette and who paid eight francs a day. Other guests' birthdays were not celebrated at the Villa. Only Madame Gendron might have been eligible, as she paid even more, but in her case it was pointless, since such nonsense no longer meant anything to the old girl anyway. Nobody even knew that her name was Anne Marguerite Rose de Gendron or gave a thought to the fact that she had been chucked under the chin and called 'Meg' at a time when a generation of gentlemen long since buried and food for the worms had still worn evening dress.

The party in honour of Madame Dumoulin was distinguished from an ordinary dinner first of all by the napkins, which were not simply laid next to the plates but stood upright in the shape of elegant cardinals' hats, then by the two francs' worth of flowers adorning the guest of honour's place, and finally by a large cake with 'Antoinette' written on it in white icing sugar with a big flourish underneath. For the last three years champagne had been drunk, thanks to the shrewdness of Madame Brulot, who had managed to find a solution to the tricky problem of how to add more lustre to the proceedings and still make something out of it as a reward for her efforts. After careful consideration she had confided in Colbert, the man who was teaching Aasgaard French and had agreed the following with him. As he did every year, Monsieur Brulot was to make a short but cogent speech, immediately followed by the serving of the cake. Carried away by the general enthusiasm which was the invariable result of all this, Colbert would spontaneously treat them to a bottle of champagne, which, however, he did not have to pay for. Madame Brulot footed the bill. The other gentle-men were then morally obliged to follow Colbert's example and once they had got going everything went swimmingly. Madame paid three francs a bottle for the champagne and charged it at seven.

The first year they had got through eleven bottles, two of which were offered by Colbert and two by Monsieur Brulot, so that their four bottles set her back twelve francs. The remaining seven, on the other hand, had produced $7 \times 4 = 28$ francs' profit, meaning that the whole operation had yielded a net gain of $28-12 = 16$ francs.

The memory of the second year brought Madame Brulot nothing but the bitterest heartache. The Serbian delegation had just moved to the Villa from Sweet Home and each of the four members had ordered no fewer than five bottles.

Last year Madame Brulot had made twenty-four francs, thanks mostly to the generosity of an irrational Italian, but this year she had no great hopes. In the first place Brizard was gone, and he certainly wouldn't have minded the odd bottle or two. In addition Madame Brulot was worried about Martin, who had still not paid up, and wanted at all costs to avoid a repetition of the Serbian affair.

Martin's Polish lady friend and her mother could not do any harm – quite the contrary – as the ladies drank their share but did not have to treat, and obviously it was imperative that as much as possible be consumed.

Well, the daughter would undoubtedly be able to handle a good few glasses and, if the mother did not have toothache and got into the swing of things, she would probably keep her end up, as the old girl had most likely not tasted champagne for years. So far, so good. But Martin himself was more of a problem. She could not very well ask him to dine elsewhere that evening; however nicely she put it, it would still remain an insult, which Martin could use to pick a quarrel, and the consequences of that were hard to predict. But then, how in heaven's name was he to be prevented from taking his turn at treating everyone, without his abstention being noticed and perhaps copied by the other male members of the company? For a moment an absurd plan involving a champagne bottle filled with water had crossed Madame Brulot's mind. Next she replaced the bottle with water in it by a completely empty bottle, but soon gave up both plans as impracticable. There was nothing for it but to let Martin offer a bottle like all the others each time his turn came round. Even supposing that she were left to foot the bill for Martin's bottles – which Madame despite everything still doubted, because a little voice told her that the Martin business would turn out all right in the end – then the three of them, Colbert, her husband and Martin, would be matched by Aasgaard, Grünewald and Knidelius. So it would be bottle for bottle, and she would make three francs on a round of six. At least if all went well, because that Knidelius was such an odd bird. Aasgaard, on the other hand, she considered good for at least two and maybe even three bottles.

On the day of the party Martin was out of the house by half past seven. He looked quite smart, having put on all the best clothes he possessed. He carried a small valise and had two walking-sticks with him. Normally, Martin never went out before eleven. In the hall he had met Louise, who was just on her way to his room with rolls and coffee and asked 'if Monsieur wished to have breakfast', to which Martin had replied that he would be breakfasting in town, adding that the ladies would be able to finish off his rolls as well as their own. He had told his Polish girlfriend he was going out on business and would probably not be back for lunch. It might well be evening before he returned, as he had to go to Chartres with one of the directors of the Crédit Lyonnais bank to set up a company there to carry out some important irrigation works in the surrounding area. It was still too early to explain things in detail. He had given her a parting kiss and left. She had sensed something was in the air, as his conviction was infectious. From the other bed the mother had called out after him 'Good luck, Henri'.

'Don't worry,' Martin had replied, 'it's all more or less wrapped up. There are just a few formalities left.' And he had gestured with his hand to both of them to keep calm, like the doctor does to a convalescent patient who tries to sing when still scarcely allowed to speak. Mother and daughter had had breakfast with a wonderful feeling of contentment that they had not known for months. Before starting on her first roll the mother had said, 'You see, Marie, help comes just when one's given up all hope. Yes, God is good,' and her prayer was as sincere as that of the shipwrecked Robinson Crusoe after his miraculous rescue.

The rolls were tough, and not crispy as they should have been. They were obviously not absolutely fresh.

'Are these the kind of rolls to serve respectable people?' complained the mother, who did not have many teeth left.

'Just you wait,' her daughter consoled her, 'tomorrow or the day after, after the bill's been settled, I'll give her a piece of my mind. Who does she think she is? Pathetic little woman.'

'You mustn't be too hard on her, Marie,' said her mother soothingly. 'It's true she might have treated us with a bit more respect, but we mustn't forget that she wasn't to know that we'd come good in the end. By the way, we mustn't forget the maids, they've not had a tip for months.'

'Won't you be sorry having to leave Paris to go and live in Chartres?' asked Marie. 'Life there must be terribly provincial.'

'My dear girl,' replied her mother, 'it's not as bad as you think. Even in a provincial town there are ways of amusing oneself. Of course we'll move into a little house with a nice garden and you'll soon get to know all the right people. You'll be very pleasantly surprised. And what's so marvellous about Paris? I often feel so terribly lonely amid all the hubbub. Oh, that Henri! I was really beginning to lose heart.'

'I wasn't,' said Marie. 'I've always been certain he'd make good.'

After they had breakfasted the two of them had another nap and then got dressed for lunch.

'Henri took my watch with him,' said Marie. 'Otherwise his watch-chain would fall out of his pocket. Just as long as that director doesn't ask him the time, or he'll look pretty silly. Just imagine, with a lady's watch. Ugh, that horrid tooth powder – now we can afford some proper toothpaste tomorrow.'

When Marie was ready, she went to see Madame Brulot, who was playing with Chico in the banqueting room.

'I just wanted to tell you, Madame, that Henri will not be lunching at the Villa today,' said Marie a little haughtily, 'so you needn't lay a place for him.'

'Oh,' replied Madame Brulot evasively, lacking the courage to inquire further.

'Yes,' said Marie, 'he's gone to Chartres with the managing director of the Crédit Lyonnais to set up a company for public works.'

Madame Brulot gave a start.

'Allow me to congratulate you,' she said with some emotion. 'I'm very glad for you. But I hope that Monsieur Martin will be back early enough to dine with us, because we're celebrating Madame Dumoulin's birthday today and dinner will be something of a party.'

'I can't promise you,' said Marie. 'Henri said it might be evening before he got back, he wasn't any more precise than that.'

'It would be a great shame,' said Madame Brulot, 'but in any case I shall certainly be counting on yourself and your mother being there.'

'I'll talk to Mama about it,' promised Marie with friendly dignity, remembering her mother's plea not to be too hard on Madame Brulot.

XIV

The Oranges

La torture par l'espérance[16]
– VILLIERS DE L'ISLE-ADAM

That evening the dining-room had a festive look. Antoinette Dumoulin had been seated next to Monsieur Brulot, and Madame Gendron was tucked safely between Brulot and his wife, who both kept an eye on her during the meal and when necessary took turns in guiding her hand towards her mouth. Mademoiselle de Kerros had been put in her old place between Aasgaard and the empty chair, and Marie sat next to her mother from force of habit, as before Martin's success had rectified the situation the two Polish women had felt in a stronger position near each other than seated separately among the other guests.

By Madame Dumoulin's plate stood a vase of roses, and the napkins had been placed upright. A clean tablecloth had even been provided, although it was only halfway through the week. Next to each plate was a menu card, handwritten by Madame Brulot herself, and reading as follows:

VILLA DES ROSES

10 Mai   Vive Antoinette!

MENU
Potage persan
Riz de veau à la Gendron
Turbot sauce Martin
Filet de bœuf à la norvégienne
Suprême de poularde hongroise
Asperges en branches à la javanaise
Meringues de Breslau
Glace à la Colbert
Fruits
Dessert
Gâteau diplomatique

It saddened Mademoiselle de Kerros to see that there was nothing *à la Kerros* or *à la bretonne,* and she would have settled for the fruit or the dessert. She could tell in all kinds of little ways that she was not liked.

Monsieur Brulot was wearing an evening jacket in which he looked quite smart, and Madame Brulot had pinned on her decorations. The two Polish women also looked impressive, Marie in a red blouse and her mother in a blue one, which they would soon be discarding now. But Aasgaard looked particularly dashing. He was all in black, with a very low-cut waistcoat and a large jewelled pin in his tie. Above his high collar his face shone with pleasure. He stood beside his chair, his right hand placed solemnly on its back, waiting for Monsieur Brulot to give the lead before sitting down. All the ladies were wearing face powder – even Marie's mother – and traces of potato-flour were visible on Madame Gendron's cheeks.

Madame Dumoulin kept them waiting a little, but at last she appeared and her evening dress was silk, as could be heard from the swish as she swept into the room. She bowed benignly and graciously and went to her place as though nothing out of the ordinary awaited her. When she saw the flowers, she said, in a tone intended to convey her utter astonishment, 'Oh, what lovely roses. Who are they in honour of, if I may ask?'

Monsieur Brulot looked at his guests and gave the appointed signal.

'*Vive Antoinette!*' rang out, and there was general applause.

Antoinette stood there as if thunderstruck, but appeared gradually to regain her composure.

'Good gracious me, so it is. I'd forgotten all about it. How terribly sweet of you.' And she thrust her nose into the flowers. Everyone laughed and came and shook hands with her in turn, Aasgaard as though in a trance, not yet fully understanding the business of birthdays, and Madame Gendron with her head nodding. Only Mademoiselle de Kerros kept her suspect hands to herself, but from her place came cries of 'Bravo, Bravo!'

Antoinette wiped away a tear, Louise served up the *Potage persan* and they all sat down. The wine was drunk almost undiluted that evening. Chico sat on Madame Brulot's right shoulder as usual, and every time he turned round his long tail swung and struck the head of Madame Gendron, who called him a 'filthy ape'. The mood was generally very animated.

After the *Turbot sauce Martin*, Monsieur Brulot got up, called for silence by tapping his knife against a glass, and said the following words:

'Ladies and gentlemen. The task I have to perform today is a much more pleasant one than that which fell to me some weeks ago after the passing of Monsieur Brizard.

'I shall be brief, ladies and gentlemen, as it is quite impossible to express in words the emotion which overwhelms us all at this moment. We are happy to be able to celebrate today, ladies and gentlemen, the birthday of someone who for years has been one of the most faithful guests at table in our Villa.

'May I express the hope that many of you will follow her example, and conclude by drinking the health of our charming companion, Madame Dumoulin, with the words "*Vive Antoinette!*" Thank you.'

While Monsieur Brulot was speaking, the guests looked down at their plates so as not to put him off, and Madame Gendron seized the opportunity to move her left arm gently along the table in the direction of a bowl of oranges which was quite close to her and represented the heading *Fruits* on the menu.

By the time Monsieur Brulot had finished, she had got far enough to be able to touch the base of the bowl with her fingertips. The master of the house sat down to thunderous applause, which made the monkey jump and the window-panes tremble, and amid this outburst Madame Gendron suddenly raised her hand, grabbed an orange and slipped it into a handbag that she always carried with her and in which, besides a handkerchief, she kept the key of her suitcase. Then she joined in the applause and said, with a benevolent laugh, 'Well spoken, my friend.'

Considering that she was ninety-two, she had accomplished the feat with considerable dexterity. But fortune did not smile on her, for Madame Brulot had seen everything.

'Watch the old girl, she's pinching oranges,' she whispered in Monsieur Brulot's ear.

The former notary thought for a moment and had a brainwave. As if to be able more easily to reach a bottle of wine that was sitting behind the oranges, he gave the bowl of fruit a shove so that it ended up much closer to Madame Gendron. Then he whispered something in Madame Brulot's ear in turn, and what he said must have been fascinating, as the news went round the table like wildfire. Every face beamed with suppressed mirth and each of them in turn cast a glance at the old woman, to see if she would fall for it. Only Aasgaard was not let into the secret. That would have involved too many technical problems and perhaps caused the whole plan to misfire, as the Norwegian would be sure to produce dictionaries and ask out loud for an explanation. Louise brought in the *Gâteau diplomatique* in both hands, putting it on display on the table until the end of dinner. When she saw the customary annual cake with her name on it Madame Dumoulin was quite overcome. Preparing herself for every eventuality she kept her handkerchief in her hand, and said with a lump in her throat:

'Dear friends, allow me to say a few heartfelt words of thanks to you for your kind gesture, which moves me more deeply than you can imagine. In Tehran my birthday was also celebrated every year, and you'll appreciate that in diplomatic circles such celebrations are attended with a good deal of ceremony. Well, you may think I'm guilty of exaggeration, for I freely admit that it must sound incredible, but I assure you that I never felt as moved out there as I do at this moment, not even on the last occasion, when the British Ambassador sat on my right. His name was Sir Douglas Westmoreland, I shall never forget it. So I thank you all again from the bottom of my heart and hope to be able to spend many more happy years among you.'

For a second time the banqueting room resounded with cheering and Madame Gendron grabbed another orange, which she put into her black velvet bag with the first. At this the cheers turned into gales of laughter, and the old woman joined in, thinking that the merriment was caused by Madame Dumoulin's speech.

'Lovely weather today, don't you think?' asked Monsieur Brulot, turning to Madame Gendron.

'It certainly is, my friend, it certainly is,' replied the old woman, 'it's very nice.'

'Do you think so? I've got a feeling, though, that there's thunder in the air,' said Brulot meaningfully.

'Do you think so?' said Madame Gendron, not taking her eyes off the dish of golden fruit. 'Yes, a storm is always a storm.'

'Do you hear, ladies and gentlemen,' said the notary, turning to the company, 'she says that a storm is always a storm, and an orange is always an orange. Well spoken, wasn't it? But she's a smart one, as she's just shown us.'

'*Un triple ban pour Madame Gendron*,' proposed Colbert.

A *triple ban* consisted of three single *bans,* each consisting of three sequences of five claps in quick succession, followed by a concluding clap, like this:

> One two three four five
> One two three four five
> One two three four five
> One,

three times in succession. The knack was to clap in perfect time, like experienced drummers, and especially to stop in unison after the single clap which followed the third sequence. Madame Gendron nodded in approval, not having been accorded such an honour for years. Colbert made a fool of himself by coming in late with an extra clap and was hooted at by the ladies.

'Monsieur Colbert,' said the youngest of the three Hungarian ladies, the one with the red lips, 'you may buy us all a drink to make up for your mistake.' It was said in a tone which made it clear that he must make up his mind quickly, as permission might otherwise be withdrawn.

Madame Brulot looked across at Colbert and he stood up. Resting his fingertips on the table, he said, with a modest smile:

'Ladies and gentlemen. I shall be delighted to accept the hint which has been so graciously given me by Her Majesty the Queen of Hungary, and therefore have the honour of offering you all a bottle of champagne.'

'Bravo, good for Monsieur Colbert!' cried Madame Brulot, and everyone joined in. Madame Gendron took her third orange, leaving nine in the dish.

'Monsieur Colbert,' warned the young Hungarian lady, 'should you again take it into your head to crown me Queen of Hungary without my permission, then I shan't hesitate to fine you a second bottle.' Without realizing it she had brushed Colbert's leg with one of her knees, and he was breathing heavily.

Madame Brulot saw just in time what was about to happen.

'No nonsense now!' she whispered to him, and Colbert controlled himself.

Madame Brulot rang, and as if by magic Louise appeared with the bottle of champagne that had been ordered, which the notary immediately took charge of.

'Bring another bottle, Louise,' he instructed. 'Ladies and gentlemen, I feel duty bound to follow the good example set by Monsieur Colbert, and hope you will accept a bottle from me too.'

'So you're trying to ruin me, are you, Monsieur?' asked Madame Brulot, wagging her finger playfully at him.

'Ruin you? No, my dearest,' replied the notary, 'but I am prepared to ruin myself for you.'

'What a gallant husband you have, Madame,' observed Madame Dumoulin approvingly.

'If he were always like that, he'd be a treasure. But I'm afraid . . .' sighed Madame Brulot, with a reproachful look at her old bed-fellow.

'Madame Malcontent,' said Brulot, 'I must point out that notaries can't very well wear themselves out the whole time with empty compliments, as that's not in keeping with the dignity of their office. But that doesn't mean they're not well disposed towards the ladies, even though ladies aren't even allowed to witness documents.'

Meanwhile, Louise had brought in the second bottle, and the fourteen glasses could now be filled. Madame Gendron especially was given a good glassful, as Brulot was sure that a generous helping of champagne would make her even bolder.

They all stood up to drink a toast, except for the old woman, who could not stand up without being pushed back from the table, chair and all. She also raised her glass to her lips, though before she had got halfway she had spilled most of it.

'For God's sake,' said Brulot, with a rueful look at the tablecloth.

'Hortense, help her with it, or she'll slosh it all over the place. Ladies and gentlemen, I should again like to propose the health of our guest of honour, and also of Madame Gendron, the doyenne of my guests and as you all know a model of honesty and virtue, of all the ladies, of Monsieur Colbert and of the other gentlemen,' he concluded with a meaningful glance at Knidelius, Aasgaard and Grünewald.

Another cry went up, and Chico started hissing like a cat at Madame Brulot.

Grünewald felt in his pocket without anyone noticing and then went over and asked Aasgaard something in a low voice.

The latter indicated his assent with his whole body.

'You say it,' said the Norwegian.

'Madame,' said Grünewald, 'Mr Aasgaard and myself should like to offer a bottle of champagne each in our turn.'

'Long live Norway and Germany' was the cry, and this time Mademoiselle de Kerros joined in too.

Meanwhile one could see that Knidelius was thinking about something. Suddenly he pointed almost imperceptibly at one of the empty bottles and gave Madame Brulot an inquiring look. She replied by raising seven fingers and Knidelius nodded.

Louise was rung for again and Madame Brulot ordered the three bottles.

'What a shame Monsieur Martin isn't here this evening,' remarked Madame Dumoulin.

'He's gone to Chartres with the managing director of the Crédit Lyonnais,' explained Madame Brulot.

'To set up a company for all kinds of public works,' said Marie by way of clarification.

'Oh really. How interesting,' said Madame Dumoulin. 'And what kind of works, if I may ask?'

'What was it again?' asked Marie, looking at her mother. Her mother said something in Polish which probably meant that she had forgotten too.

'It wasn't imitation works,' said Marie, thinking aloud. 'Importation works . . . no, it was something else. What a nuisance. It's on the tip of my tongue and I just can't think of it.'

'It was something to do with water,' said her mother.

'It wouldn't be irrigation works by any chance?' asked Madame Dumoulin.

'That's it!' said mother and daughter together. 'To set up a company for irrigation works.'

'I thought so,' said Madame Dumoulin. 'Yes, those things are very interesting. They did a lot of that in Persia. Look, here's Tehran, and the whole area on this side was desert and they were always carrying out irrigation works in various places.'

With her knife she drew something on the white tablecloth which was supposed to represent a map of Persia.

Monsieur Brulot thought for a moment. He knew the plain near Chartres that the French call 'la Beauce'. Could that be short of water by any chance? Wasn't the soil there as fertile as in the most favoured spot on earth? But it might be south-east of Chartres and he only knew the area to the south-west. Also the situation might have changed since he had moved to Paris.

'You come from Java, don't you, Monsieur?' asked Madame Dumoulin, turning to her neighbour.

'Yes, Madame,' replied Knidelius, his cheeks beginning to burn.

'I expect there are lots of irrigation works there too?'

'Well, a few.' And from the tone of his voice it was obvious he was thinking, 'For God's sake shut up about that bloody island.'

Glasses were refilled and a toast was drunk to the success of the irrigation works. Madame Gendron removed her fourth orange.

'It's too much,' spluttered Mademoiselle de Kerros, choking on her champagne.

Monsieur decided that the moment had come.

'It's time for the oranges,' he began. 'Wait a minute, that's a funny way they're divided up; there are a lot fewer in one bowl than the other. Those maids can't even lay a table properly.' And he rang for Louise.

'Why did you put a lot fewer oranges in one dish than in the other?' asked Brulot gruffly.

'Excuse me, Monsieur, but there were twelve in each bowl,' Louise corrected him politely.

'Are you sure?'

'Quite sure, Monsieur.' She was prepared to swear to it.

'All right,' said Brulot, 'you can go. Ladies and gentlemen,' he went on, with a wink, 'it pains me to have to say that there is someone at this table who is unworthy to be part of your distinguished company. Four oranges have been stolen, and I should like the culprit to own up immediately.'

There was no answer, and everyone tried to keep a straight face. Aasgaard listened open-mouthed and with his eyes screwed up.

'The guilty person is not going to own up then,' continued Monsieur Brulot. 'Ladies and gentlemen, in order to protect the innocent from suspicion, there is nothing for it but for us all to allow our pockets to be checked. Madame Brulot can look after the ladies and I'll look after the gentlemen. Does any of you object to this suggestion?'

All the guests shook their heads, including Madame Gendron, who now realized what a narrow escape she had had. For if she had put the oranges in her dress pocket instead of in her handbag, the game would have been up.

The search began immediately.

'I propose that Monsieur Brulot searches the ladies and Madame Brulot the gentlemen,' shouted Colbert, rubbing his nose.

'Heavens, no,' protested one of the Hungarian girls, glancing at the master of the house.

'It's just Monsieur Colbert's little joke,' said the notary, reassuring her.

Monsieur and Madame Brulot then pretended to conduct a thorough search, but found nothing.

'Ladies and gentlemen,' said the notary, 'the search has not produced any result. Only Madame Gendron has not been searched, but it goes without saying that this venerable lady cannot be responsible. She at least is above all suspicion.' Madame Gendron looked at him gratefully. 'However, should you insist that she be searched too, even if only for form's sake, then she is of course prepared for her pockets to be examined.'

'I've only got one pocket,' the old woman corrected him.

'Amendment noted,' said Monsieur Brulot. 'Then she is of course prepared for her pocket to be searched,' he corrected himself.

Madame Gendron let her handbag slip gently to the floor and pushed it a little way under the table with her foot.

'I don't think there should be any exceptions in a case like this,' said Madame Dumoulin.

'Of course not,' said Colbert. '*Liberté, Égalité, Fraternité.*' And he launched into the 'Marseillaise'.

'Madame,' said Brulot, pulling the chair with the old woman on it away from the table, 'could I ask you to stand up for a second. It won't take a moment.'

Madame Gendron did as she was asked, and pointed out her pocket herself. Madame Brulot felt in it and declared it to be empty.

'Madame,' said Brulot, 'we are most obliged to you for your co-operation. I only hope you won't hold it against us; there was really no alternative. Won't you sit down again, Madame Gendron?' And with a gallant gesture he invited her to be seated.

The old woman's features relaxed, and a feeling of immense relief transfigured her face as she sank back into her chair.

Monsieur Brulot made as if to push her back into her place, when he suddenly bent down, crawled a little way under the table and emerged with a green velvet bag.

'You mustn't let this fall on the floor, Madame,' he said, handing her the bag.

Madame Gendron reached out for it despairingly with both hands.

'Wait a moment,' said Brulot, 'I'm going to give you a present. I haven't given you one for ages and little gifts help keep up a friendship.'

He picked the handsomest orange of the eight still left in the bowl and opened the bag to put it in. The old woman sat there as though petrified, smiling in desperation.

Suddenly a look of utter astonishment appeared on Monsieur Brulot's face.

'Dear God in heaven,' he stammered, 'what's this?' And he immediately took the bag by two corners and emptied it out on to the table. There lay the handkerchief, the key and the four stolen oranges. Brulot took off his black cap as though he were at a graveside. A huge roar of laughter went through the banqueting room and Madame Gendron's lower lip trembled as though she were murmuring the Lord's Prayer. She looked in turn at the master of the house, her fellow-guests and the four ghastly oranges, and the little blood that she had left rushed to her cheeks. She was ashamed.

'Ladies and gentlemen,' said Brulot, 'the mystery of the stolen oranges has been solved, and there sits the culprit, who exposed you all to suspicion. We really ought to hand her over to the police, but we won't, in order to spare her a twenty-year sentence. On the other hand I propose that we divide her fortune, which according to Monsieur Garousse amounts to two million francs, between us. Someone who steals oranges is capable of stealing other things and can't have come by her money honestly. It stands to reason that she must forfeit it.'

The mention of the word fortune seemed to get through to the old woman, who suddenly stood up so that her grey head looked down on the seated gathering.

'It's a lie,' she blurted out, grabbing the bag, the key and the handkerchief, 'I've got less than fourteen thousand francs left. I had to pay for a new dress only the other day.'

'Now listen to me,' said Monsieur Brulot, 'the money passes to us. The papers have already been drawn up.' And he produced a newspaper from his inside pocket.

'Just you dare!' screamed Madame Gendron, gripping the key tighter in her fist as though about to lash out with it. 'Thieves, frauds, rabble!' she shouted, leaving the banqueting room entirely unaided.

'Ladies and gentlemen,' said Brulot, raising his voice so as to be heard by the old woman as she left, 'the division of the estate will take place tomorrow morning at ten o'clock in my office, 71 rue d'Armaillé.'

The old woman stopped in the doorway and turned round. Then she raised her fist at everyone sitting round the table, spat on the ground as a sign of deep contempt and disappeared into the hall. Chico clenched his fist and threatened her back.

Monsieur Brulot replaced the oranges in the bowl in a neat pile.

XV

And You'll Soon Get to Know All the Right People

Colbert, Brulot, Aasgaard and Grünewald had each ordered another bottle of champagne. Knidelius, however, went on drinking, but stared straight ahead of him and did not say another word.

So that nine bottles were all they were going to have, making a profit of eight francs, and anyway it was time that the drinking came to an end, as everyone was beginning to behave oddly. Madame Dumoulin had taken a rose out of her bouquet and stuck it in Monsieur Brulot's buttonhole, and Madame Brulot was busily engaged in explaining to Colbert why she would *much* rather have been a man than a woman.

'Perhaps we went a bit too far,' piped up Mademoiselle de Kerros unexpectedly, thinking back on all she had had to endure over the years on account of her lame foot. 'We should have told her it was just a joke before she left.'

Monsieur Brulot, who took the remark as a personal insult, gave her a withering look.

'When you've reached my age, Mademoiselle, then you will, I hope, understand all these things much better,' he replied in a sympathetic tone. Then, turning to the others with a shrug of his shoulders and paying no further attention to her, he said, 'One's got to teach the old girl a good lesson every now and again, otherwise we won't be able to do a thing with her. That woman . . . but I'd better not go on, or else I'll never stop.'

In such a large gathering there are always a few advocates of Christian charity, and Madame Brulot was afraid that the fun might turn sour. Before anyone could say another word she banged on the table and said that Colbert must sing something.

Colbert cleared his throat so amusingly that the ladies and

gentlemen, with the exception of Aasgaard, were breathless with laughter.

'What would the ladies like me to sing?' he asked in a nasal voice which would have been the making of him if he had been a professional comic. 'Something serious or something . . .'

'Something amusing,' requested Madame Brulot.

'That's easily said. Amusing. But *what? Tous les soldats du régiment?*'

'No, that's corny. Don't you know anything else?'

'*Ayez pitié d'elle?* But I'm afraid . . .'

'Don't be silly,' protested Madame Brulot. 'We're not children any more, I should have thought. Off you go.'

'But don't take it *too* far,' warned Antoinette Dumoulin.

Mademoiselle de Kerros, who had very soon forgiven and forgotten everything, offered to accompany him. That was of course even better and so Mademoiselle sat down at the piano. Colbert hummed the tune and the pianist quickly got the hang of it. First she struck two high chords, then two low ones and finally two in the middle range which were suitable for a man's voice. She gave a 'so mi, so mi' introduction, and Colbert began.

The song was a husband's lament at the physical transformations undergone by his wife over the years. In turn he compared her various parts with how they had been when she was young. The poor creature had obviously not improved with age, as each verse ended with the refrain:

Ayez pipi, ayez pipitié d'elle.[17]

The ambiguity of *pipi* amused the gathering immensely, especially the verse in which it was said of her poor breasts that the nipples were:

> *. . . et tout ratatinés,*
> *On les prendrait pour deux choux de Bruxelles,*[18]
> *Ayez pipi, ayez pipitié d'elle.*

On that memorable evening Colbert surpassed himself, for as he was being applauded he thought up a last verse on the spur of the moment, which went down even better than anything he had achieved so far. It ended with the words:

> *Voilà l'histoire de Madame Gendronelle,*[19]
> *Ayez pipi, ayez pipitié d'elle.*

'Why don't you sing something,' whispered the Polish woman to her daughter in encouragement, 'you know, that ballad.'

'All I know is the one about the madman, *L'Insensé*,' protested Marie feebly.

'That's the one,' said her mother, 'that's a lot better than what that chap over there has just been giving us. Come on, when someone's got a lovely voice like you they've simply got to sing. In a minute all the others will be starting and you won't get a look-in. You know what they're like, everything for themselves and nothing for anyone else.'

Meanwhile, Mademoiselle de Kerros was playing Grieg's *Morgenstimmung* as well as she could from memory, as she knew he was a compatriot of Aasgaard's. The Norwegian heard the familiar melody and began whistling along. Mademoiselle de Kerros smiled.

Then Marie began humming the opening notes of *L'Insensé*. The pianist immediately struck up the accompaniment and asked if she knew the words.

'I think I do more or less,' said Marie casually, 'although one forgets these things terribly quickly.'

'Off you go,' cried Mademoiselle de Kerros, becoming enthusiastic, 'come on and sing. Whatever you like.' And she ran her fingers over the keys at lightning speed, from the thunderous bass notes on the left all the way to the other end.

'All things considered she doesn't play too badly,' said Madame Dumoulin to Monsieur Brulot. 'A shame about the way she looks.' She had half closed her eyes and was keeping time with her foot on the floor.

'Yes, the *Insensé* is a very beautiful romance,' said the young Hungarian lady.

'Get on with it,' growled Marie's mother, 'that Hungarian girl knows it too.'

'Well, Madame, let's hear you,' was Brulot's kind invitation.

'Oh,' spluttered Marie.

'Whether you like it or not, you're going to sing,' cajoled Madame Brulot. 'This evening you're ours and that means we can use your talents as we see fit. All the more so since that heartless Monsieur Martin will soon be whisking you off.'

'I really can't help it,' sighed Marie, 'and I assure you we shall be sorry to leave you all. Mama and I aren't at all keen on higher circles, where generally all one can expect is jealousy and malicious gossip.' Her mother nodded in agreement.

'You're perfectly right,' said Madame Dumoulin, 'and I know what I'm talking about. Of course there are a few nice people, you find them everywhere, but they're oh so scarce! That Sir Douglas, for example, was a real gentleman. But you'll probably be better off, because I believe that financial circles are in general less corrupt than the diplomatic world, which I moved in for years and which I know through and through, believe me.'

'I sincerely hope so,' said Marie, 'Mama and I don't like intrigues.'

'On with the show!' cried Mademoiselle de Kerros, whereupon Marie took up her position next to the pianist. It went quiet around the table. They heard Mademoiselle count softly to three, after which Marie's voice rang out bravely:

> *Dans ce lieu sombre,*
> *Et tout rempli d'effroi,*
> *Quelle est cette ombre,*
> *Toujours là, devant moi?*[20]

This song was as touching as Colbert's had been malicious. It concerned a man who was locked up in a madhouse and saw the ghost of his beloved hovering in front of him day and night. The company were immediately enthralled, but it was a mournful tune too.

Between the first and second verses Louise came in on tiptoe and handed a letter to Madame Brulot. 'An express letter for Madame.' Madame Brulot cast a peevish glance at Monsieur. How stupid of Louise. The letter was from Boulogne-sur-Mer. How ridiculous!

Boulogne-sur-Mer! But as it was an express letter, she opened it at once, as one never knew. Marie sang:

> *Ton front si pur portait une couronne*
> *Faite des fleurs de tes jeunes printemps.*[21]

Suddenly Madame Brulot tied the monkey to her chair and left the banqueting room, obviously overcome by intense emotion. Monsieur Brulot frowned and followed her with his gaze. Everyone realized that something terrible had happened, except for Marie and Mademoiselle de Kerros, who had their backs turned to the company and had not noticed a thing.

Louise appeared and interrupted the singing by asking 'if the Polish ladies would mind coming along to see Madame Brulot in the office'.

'Tell Madame I'll be finished in just a moment,' said Marie, resuming her song:

> *Dieu, repoussez cette âme criminelle,*
> *Qui profana ses serments et sa foi.*[22]

Louise came in again, this time flustered and red in the face, bearing the message 'that Madame wished to speak to the two ladies immediately'. They obeyed her request.

A moment later the sound of a short altercation was heard, followed by muffled sobbing, which penetrated from the office into the banqueting room. The members of the company looked at each other. Monsieur Brulot growled something and left the table, anxious to find out what was going on. In the office he found mother and daughter sitting together. In front of them stood his wife, pale and with a letter in her hand.

'What's going on?' asked Brulot in a commanding tone but with death in his heart.

'Mind your own business,' Madame snapped at him, looking helplessly out of the window into the garden.

'I want to know what's going on,' Brulot insisted, suspecting that his wife was in need of help and consolation.

'There you are, take it!' she cried, throwing the letter at him.

Monsieur Brulot picked it up and began reading. It was a communication from Martin telling Madame Brulot that force of circumstances had obliged him to set sail for America. He hoped to make his fortune there, and when he did would repay Madame Brulot everything he owed her, 'as God is my judge'. In order to avoid arguments and unpleasantness which might easily arise at a later stage, he gave in his letter the following detailed breakdown of the amount due, and Madame Brulot had to admit that he had calculated everything generously.

A. Lodging:

December	31 days
January	31 "
February	28 "
March	31 "
April	30 "
May	10 "

Total . . . 161 days @ F14.00 . . . . F2,254.00

B. Laundry:
@ F5.00 per month for myself
and F10.00 per month for each of the ladies,
Total F25.00 per month . . . F133.33
in round figures 134.00

C. Soap, candles, etc. 15.00

D. For the maids
@ F5.00 per month each,
including May 60.00

TOTAL F2,463.00

In round figures let's say F2,465.00 (two thousand four hundred and sixty-five francs), on which sum he would pay compound interest at a rate of five per cent per annum from now until the day of settlement.

Finally he commended Marie and her mother to the protection of Madame Brulot and the letter was signed: Yours sincerely, HENRI MARTIN.

Monsieur broke into nervous laughter. Madame continued staring out of the window. Marie was crying and the tears were falling on to her red blouse. Her eyes and cheeks were smudged and, fat as she was, she looked utterly pitiful. She had not only lost in Martin her sole means of support, but his departure also spelt the end of her last great love. The mother sat huddled against her daughter, less broad, less fat and generally more decrepit. Her feet scarcely touched the floor, seeing as she was very short, and she kept her hands folded.

'Ah, the swine, *le misérable!*' exploded Brulot. 'Ah! *nom de Dieu!* If I ever meet the bloke again I'll break every bone in his body, or my name's not Brulot. I was quite right to wonder since when the plain of Beauce was in need of water. What a villain. I'll give him irrigation works, the scoundrel.'

And rounding on the two women, he barked:

'Off you go, you two, pack your things and get out.'

'Christ, if only you were a man instead of a slut,' he hissed at Marie, clenching his fists, and one could see that it was a cause of real regret.

Mother and daughter left the office, Marie in front and her mother following on behind. The old woman closed her eyes as she crossed the threshold, expecting a terrible kick up the backside. The guests were crowded together in the banqueting room and were looking into the hall. Aline and Louise were peering through the kitchen door and each of them was trying to push the other forward.

The two Polish women went up to the room where the three of them had spent so many happy days, and Marie looked helplessly at all the mess, wondering what to pack first. Brulot stood at the door and watched her.

Then the mother asked something in Polish that Brulot could not understand, whereupon Marie took their joint purse out of her pocket and carefully counted its contents.

The dull sound of the copper change and the two half-franc coins – such coins don't jingle – caused Brulot to approach.

'Let's have a look,' he said, 'how much money have you got?'

Marie handed over the purse, and now Brulot counted it in his turn. There was one franc forty in it.

'What about you, granny?' he asked, turning to the mother.

The latter understood his meaning immediately and simply turned out her pocket.

Then Brulot again thought of the two thousand four hundred odd francs, and he flung the purse down on the table. A few five-centime pieces rolled out and, after some hunting about on all fours, were recovered by Marie and her mother.

Brulot next went over and fingered the clothes on the hatstand. However, the results were disappointing and, averting his head as though he were going to be sick, he said, 'Bah, bloody rags!'

In the corner there was an old trunk.

'Open it up,' ordered the notary.

Marie obeyed and Brulot disappeared into it from the waist upwards. For a second it occurred to Marie that it only needed one good push to tip him right into it, but she was so despondent she could not even raise a smile.

Brulot's examination was brief but thorough, like a customs officer's. There really wasn't anything worth impounding.

Meanwhile, Madame Brulot had told the guests what had happened, and they all realized that there was no question of any further celebrations that evening. They all dispersed and Madame came up to see what her husband was up to.

The notary was just emerging from the trunk.

'I've made an inventory and you can save yourself the trouble of looking,' said Brulot. 'They haven't got a thing, not a thing. As far as I'm concerned they can keep the rubbish, it's so filthy I wouldn't touch it with a bargepole. Just make sure they get out right away.'

And turning to the maids, who were still standing by the kitchen door, he said, 'Which of you let him out?'

'What do you mean, Monsieur, let him out?' asked Louise, because no one was ever 'let out', since all the guests were free to come and go as they pleased.

'What do you mean, Monsieur, what do you mean,' snarled Brulot. 'Don't you two understand French any more? Who saw him leave?'

Aline nudged Louise.

'This morning as I was taking up breakfast I met Monsieur in the hall,' said Louise.

'And didn't it occur to you that it was very early to be going out for a walk?'

'Goodness me, no, Monsieur.'

'You stupid bloody girl,' cursed Brulot. 'And didn't he say anything?'

'Monsieur just said he'd be breakfasting in town.'

'And didn't you notice anything about him? Didn't he have anything with him?'

'No, Monsieur. Just the brown valise and two walking-sticks.'

'Two walking-sticks?' asked Brulot. 'Two?'

'Yes,' said Louise, 'the bamboo one he always took with him and the one with the silver handle.'

The notary turned away in disgust.

'He had two walking-sticks with him, Monsieur,' he erupted, buttonholing the Norwegian, who had just come downstairs to get something. 'Two walking-sticks, do you understand? And people find that quite natural here and that wretched maid lets a bloke like that just escape, after first having a chat with him.' Then Brulot turned on his heel, walked to his room and slammed the door behind him, without worrying about Chico, who was left sitting all alone by the large table in the banqueting room.

All this fuss upset Madame Brulot, notwithstanding the stabbing pain of the two thousand four hundred and sixty-five francs. Preferring not to watch, she went to the kitchen.

Marie and her mother crammed the greater part of their possessions into the trunk and made a parcel of the best remaining items.

When they had finished they put on their hats.

The mother went over to the window and pressed her face against the glass, in order to look out into the garden. The clock of the chapel on the corner struck eleven. It looked far from inviting outside, the air being very raw although it was May. It was so bad that a fire had been lit in the banqueting room for the past few days. The two women hesitated and looked at each other.

'Where are we going to sleep?' asked the old woman.

'I really don't know,' said Marie.

There *are* places in Paris where two people can spend the night for one franc, but those establishments are not very suitable for women and certainly not for unaccompanied ladies, besides which neither of them knew of such an address. And it was too late by now to look for another family boarding-house. For that matter, for the first time in their lives they did not even dare do that at that moment. They were utterly demoralized and only now realized fully that with Martin's departure they had lost all prestige. The three of them might have been able to carry it off, but now there was no chance. With Martin, broad-backed and bespectacled, leading the way and the two of them following on modestly behind, they had been able to gain admittance wherever they wanted. Martin did the talking, and all they had to do was stroke a dog or give a few centimes to a child. But without him they had lost the old confidence which ensured success everywhere.

Mother and daughter were now ready. They listened and heard a door shut upstairs. Must be someone going to bed. In the kitchen people were talking softly.

'Where's Monsieur?' asked the mother in a whisper.

'Gone to bed, I think,' replied Marie.

'And Madame?'

'In the kitchen with the maids.'

They both listened in silence again. They broke into a sweat.

'Marie!'

'What is it?'

'Won't you try asking Madame if we can sleep here for tonight? It won't cost her a sou, as the room will be standing empty anyway.'

'I'd rather you asked,' said Marie, 'you're older and you'll make more of an impression.'

'No,' objected the mother. 'My French isn't good enough. I'd give it a try if I were you. She can only say no. You've got to, otherwise where are we supposed to go?'

'All right,' agreed Marie, 'but let's wait till she comes to us. I'd rather not go to the kitchen with a request like that. Louise is all right, but that Aline, with that impudent look of hers . . .'

Mother and daughter leant against the bed and kept quiet. No one came. 'Hum,' coughed the old woman to attract attention, unable to keep her eyes open any longer.

'Go and see what they're getting up to, and check if they're nearly ready yet,' asked Madame Brulot.

Louise went very reluctantly and asked politely 'whether the ladies were ready'.

Marie plucked up all her courage.

'Listen, Louise. Will you do something for us? I know you've not had a tip for a few months . . .'

'What can I do for you, Madame?'

'Ask Madame Brulot if we can sleep here. It's nearly half past eleven and there's nowhere for us to go. And come to that, we haven't got enough money for a hotel bed,' she admitted honestly. 'And it won't cost Madame Brulot a thing, as the room will be empty anyway,' she added, to give Louise an argument to use in case Madame Brulot raised objections.

Louise went to the kitchen to deliver the message.

'Well?' asked Madame Brulot.

'They're ready, Madame. But they're asking whether they can spend the night here, as they haven't got enough money for a hotel.'

Madame Brulot looked round at the door of her room. She could hear the floorboards creaking beneath the feet of her husband, who must be getting undressed. Throwing the Polish women out on the street in the middle of the night and without a sou in their pockets was something she would rather not have on her conscience. But she was afraid of the sarcasm of the old notary, who would be sure to curse and make fun of her if she dared give in.

Aline had caught Madame Brulot's glance and realized that she was undecided.

'You're talking as though Madame would dare decide without asking Monsieur's permission,' said Aline to Louise, just loud enough for Madame Brulot to hear. The latter's vanity was wounded.

'All right then,' she decided immediately, 'they can stay at the

Villa for tonight. And give them a cup of coffee and a couple of rolls tomorrow morning, Louise . . . For heaven's sake, what do a few more francs matter?' she concluded with a sigh.

That night the notary refused to have anything to do with Chico in bed.

'I believe the old woman's got another daughter and a couple of sons living in Poland,' scoffed Brulot. 'Why don't you sell all your furniture, and then you can bring them over too.'

'Just you make sure that your case gets settled, you lazy old devil,' Madame snapped back.

'Keep your filthy monkey to yourself, or I'll wring its neck,' said Brulot, taking a swipe at Chico but deliberately missing him, as he loved the creature almost as much as his wife did. The monkey jumped into Madame Brulot's arms at a bound, from where it began hissing indignantly at the notary.

'Come here, mummy's darling,' said Madame Brulot comfortingly, hugging the creature to her bosom. 'If he dares raise so much as a finger to you, he'll get a chain round his neck too.' And to her husband she said, 'Have you got that, you big bully? You're disgusting.' Whereupon she turned her back on him.

'Ha, ha, ha! He's going to pay interest on the interest!' chuckled Brulot, 'that's a good one.'

XVI

The Visit

Unless they were having a tiff, Louise was busy in Richard's room by seven in the morning. She would brush his clothes, darn his socks, change his handkerchief and put everything in its place, as the man was incapable of doing a thing for himself. And so as not to disturb his sleep she would take off her slippers when she had to move about the room.

Breakfast for guests who paid only five francs a day consisted of a cup of coffee and two rolls. But the coffee was bad, because Aline made it the night before so she could lie in longer in the mornings. Since Richard had complained to Louise about this, he got a lovely cup of tea and occasionally hot chocolate in the mornings, depending on the whims of Madame Dumoulin, as only she was entitled to them. And he no longer got two rolls, but as many as four or five, which Grünewald could easily tackle, as Germans are used to heavy breakfasts. Madame Brulot would be unlikely to notice the tea or cocoa, because they were in large tins which lasted for a long time and made effective control impossible.

But those wretched rolls, which the Kraut demolished in one bite, had her in a constant panic.

At half past seven Louise would sit on the edge of the bed in order to be able to enjoy contemplating him from a comfortable position, and at twenty-five to eight she would wake him with a kiss on the mouth. And even if he sometimes smelled of the previous evening's beer, each time was as wonderful as the time before. As he opened his eyes, she would whisper, '*Bonjour*, Richard' and he would reply:

'*Bonjour*, Louisette.'

As soon as Grünewald left, Louise went back to his room to

clear away the remains of breakfast and eliminate at once all traces
of tea or chocolate. Sometimes she would stretch out full length on
the bed, sniffing in the smell of the sheets he had slept in and biting
the pillow where his head had rested.

She thought of him till he came home at lunchtime, and all afternoon too. When Madame was out at her Poor Relief Committee
and Monsieur was going through his files in the banqueting room
with Chico on his shoulder, Aline and Louise would sometimes
stand at the kitchen window peering out into the street. And whenever any gentlemen passed by, Louise would compare the suits they
were wearing, the length of their moustaches and the colour of
their hair, with Richard's suit, moustache and hair. All the younger
men were wearing high double collars which fitted so wonderfully
around the neck, but Richard still wore those long, old-fashioned
single collars, which left the Adam's apple showing. And when she
thought of that, tears would well up in Louise's eyes, she found it so
endearing. Dear Richard!

Every other evening they would go for a walk, but three times a
week Grünewald had to go to the German Club for a beer and a
game of skittles. When it was fine they would go into the Bois de
Boulogne, and when it rained they would sit on the terrace of some
abandoned café near the old city walls. Louise would rest her head
on his shoulder and look ecstatically at everything about him, even
the hair growing out of his nostrils. Now and then she would tease
him by grabbing his arm as he was about to raise his glass to his lips,
or tickling his leg when he least expected it. And he could tell from
her suppressed laughter how much she was enjoying herself.
Whenever a visitor or a waiter came past, Grünewald would warn
her to be careful, but Louise was deaf, dumb and blind. He used
the argument that one of the guests from the Villa might come past
and that it would be better for her if nobody knew about them;
because he did not dare admit that he was a little ashamed, since
she looked so much like a maid.

Every other Sunday afternoon they would go to St-Cloud, a
small town nearby, where there was a large wood.[23] They would
leave the footpaths and do their best to get lost. In some place
where there was nothing to be seen except thick undergrowth all

around they would sit down and frolic on the grass. And Louise was oblivious to the gnats, however spitefully they bit her through her stockings. Sometimes they would be angry with each other and would not speak for hours on end. After they had made love, Grünewald would sometimes try to teach her a few words of German, to pass the time. She could already say '*ich liebe dich*' and '*eins zwei drei*',[24] however odd her pronunciation, and next he tried to teach her to tackle '*bis zum Tode getreu*' in one breath.

'Come on, try it again. *Bis – zum – To – de – ge – treu –*.' Word by word, and each time he would give her a tap with a branch he had broken off.

'What does it mean?' asked Louise.

'Faithful unto death.'

'Is that true, Richard?'

'Of course, ask any German.'

'Oh, you. I meant if you really will be.'

'Be what?'

'That.'

'Faithful unto death? Why not? But that's not the point now. Come on, one word at a time, *Bis – zum – . . .*' After a quarter of an hour she knew it by heart and kept saying 'me *bis zum Tode getreu,* you not *bis zum Tode getreu,*' till Richard got angry and started giving her dirty looks.

He could not help occasionally asking her about her first husband.

Grünewald was a little jealous of the stranger and wanted to know if he had been tall; if he had worn a beard; if he had been strong; if he, Grünewald, would still have become her lover even if she had not lost her husband; what illness he had died of; and finally, which of them she loved or had loved most, as the case might be. When Louise said that her husband had been tall, Richard laughed rather mockingly, as if to say that his height had not helped him much, and when she assured him that he had also been physically strong the German felt his biceps without her noticing. In reply to the question what he had died of, Louise replied 'consumption'. And Grünewald became a little uneasy, since he had already coughed three or four times that day. When he finally asked which of the two she loved most deeply, Louise refused to answer at first, thinking to herself that it was too unequal a match.

'Come on,' Richard urged her bitterly, 'go ahead and say it. You don't have to spare my feelings. Him, don't you?'

Louise was silent.

'I thought as much,' he said.

'I didn't say so, did I?'

'No, but you don't have to. I know everything.'

'Well then, you've got it all wrong.'

'You're just saying that. You're not going to tell me you love me best?'

'Yes I am,' said Louise softly. And it was the truth. The dead man was so dead and the other so warm and alive. And Richard said he didn't believe her, but was glad nevertheless.

Late in the afternoon, as the church bells were tolling, they descended the steep streets that led down to the river and took the boat back to Paris. There were all kinds of people on board: couples standing silently in corners, groups of young people kicking up a fuss and sitting on the railings because it was forbidden, solitary gentlemen with wrinkled eyelids who kept their left hands in their pockets and leered at the girls through the smoke of their cigarettes. Dusk fell and here and there on the banks gas lamps were lit.

They got off the boat in the centre of town and went in search of a suitable restaurant. First they would walk up and down past the windows to see if it looked respectable but not too expensive, and then Richard would push her inside with a movement of his hip.

They would sit down at a table for two, and Louise would be given the menu and chose the dishes while Richard ordered wine. She also tossed the salad and cut his meat for him from force of habit, and also partly to show him that she was not idle and would make him a good wife, as he might one day contemplate marriage after all. You never knew.

The two of them could usually eat for five francs, including wine, and Richard would pay the waiter with a heavy heart. As a budding businessman it struck him that they might just as well eat at the Villa, where it cost nothing as he paid monthly anyway, and Louise was also entitled to eat at Madame Brulot's on Sunday. It was just that they couldn't eat together at one table there, as Richard – being a guest – ate in the banqueting room, while Louise had to go to the kitchen.

Still, there was a lot to be said for it, thought Grünewald. Because paying out five francs just for the pleasure of rubbing knees, especially when they had already spent a whole afternoon together, was really too much of a good thing.

After dinner they would go to a *café-chantant*, where they each spent two hours over one drink, as there was nothing to be had for less than a franc. Ladies with plunging necklines would sing songs, and there would be French soldiers with dented caps and red noses. And the words were just a riot. On the way home Louise would still be giggling. 'Do you really think it was all that funny?' Richard would ask.

At this period Grünewald was truly lord and master, and day by day everyone else, living or dead, lost ground in Louise's heart. She had only realized it herself when her brother and little boy had paid her a surprise visit one Sunday afternoon when she was due to go out with Grünewald. Louise was busy fastening her corset in her bedroom when the two unfortunates entered the kitchen where Aline was mopping the floor. Her brother immediately put his finger to his lips to stop Aline giving the game away by screaming or something, and then asked her just to call out 'that there were two gentlemen to see the widow Louise Créteur'.

'What's that?' asked Louise.

'There are two gentlemen here who'd like to speak to you,' repeated Aline.

They could hear Louise's voice repeating 'Two gentlemen?' under her breath, while Aline motioned to the visitors to hide under the table, where she had already mopped up.

They both crawled into the place she had indicated.

'Careful now,' said the brother to her son, who had knocked the box of cakes with his head.

Louise now had enough clothes on to be presentable.

'What's all this about gentlemen?' she asked Aline, who was still mopping so that only her legs were visible.

These words were greeted with a burst of joyous laughter, and arms and heads appeared from under the table.

Louise, realizing who it was, shot a glance at the alarm clock. It had just turned three, and at half past three she was due to meet Richard on the corner.

Meanwhile Lucien had got to his feet and thrown his arms round his mother.

She kissed him on both cheeks, on his forehead and on his ears, till it made his little head spin, for she loved him very much. Her brother stood a few paces off and kept the box of cakes hidden behind his back. Then he too was given a kiss, as is the French custom, and explained how everything had come about. He had been given four days' leave by his colonel, of which two were almost over, so that he had to report back on Tuesday evening. That morning he had suddenly had the idea of paying her a surprise visit, and had gone to fetch Lucien in Rambouillet, as he so loved taking the train. And here they were. He laughed, gave her the box of cakes, and passed on the regards of the whole village.

'You've forgotten that NCO who tried to cancel your leave,' said Lucien.

Louise listened as well as she could, keeping her eye on the alarm clock all the while. Seventeen minutes past three. Thirteen minutes left. If only he would wait a bit.

'What are all those pots for, Mummy?' asked Lucien, who had never seen so much kitchen equipment in one place.

'To cook with, lad,' said Aline, as this was her department.

'But you can't put them all on top of that stove?'

'No, not all at once.'

'What's in that drawer?'

'All sorts of things. Knives, forks, spoons.'

'And what's that cupboard for?'

Grünewald came downstairs and left the house, a sign that it was time.

'For putting nosy little boys in,' said Louise.

Turning to her brother, she said, 'What a shame you didn't write in advance and tell me you were coming, then we'd have been able to go out together.'

'Aren't you free then?'

'No, not really,' she replied, fiddling with Lucien's collar. 'At least, I promised an old lady who lives in the boarding-house that I'd take her for a walk for an hour or two. She hardly ever gets out, poor old dear.'

'Well, anyway, we've seen you,' said her brother.

'What time were you thinking of going back to Rambouillet?'

'About seven.'

'Now, look. It's only three. You can't walk around all that time. No, I won't have that. I'll go and tell the old dear . . . But do you know what you can do? Take Lucien to the cinema. You like films, don't you, son?'

'Smashing,' said Lucien.

'There's a nice place just round the corner, isn't there, Aline?'

'In avenue de Wagram,'[25] said Aline. 'In fact there are two.'

'Wait a minute.' And Louise went to her room.

Lucien tugged at his uncle's sleeve.

'What is it?'

'Mummy's gone to get some money.'

'Shush now,' said his uncle, looking the other way.

Louise quickly returned and gave her brother three francs in silver and a whole pile of change. Lucien received a half franc. Her brother saluted and said 'Thank you, captain.'

Laughing, Lucien copied him. Then they said goodbye.

Louise hugged Lucien fiercely.

'Be a good boy now.'

Turning to her brother she said:

'Give mother and father a hug from me. And Jeanne and Mariette, and Pierre.'

She cast a final glance at her son.

'And make sure Lucien gets a haircut. But not out of his half franc, mind!'

The two of them left and Louise watched from the kitchen window. They turned round once more and the large figure got the small one to wave his hand. Louise waved back. Finally they turned the corner. It was 3.37.

'Hurry up,' said Aline, 'or Madame Gendron will leave without you.'

Louise did not reply. She hurriedly put on her hat, grabbed her umbrella and rushed down the street to where Richard was standing waiting for her. And when she caught sight of him from a distance she realized that she had no son, no father and mother, no village and no past any more, but that she had a man of flesh and blood, who could kiss and was a king and who was waiting over there, on two legs, just like any ordinary mortal.

XVII

Revenge

When Madame Gendron got back to her room after leaving the banqueting room, she saw oranges dancing in the dark. She could not get to sleep that night, as the thought that Brulot was after her money, and that the papers were already drawn up, would not leave her in peace. At about half past ten Louise had come up to help her into bed. But the old woman, whom she found sitting in her chair, had given her such a filthy look that she had quickly gone down-stairs again.

Madame Gendron sat there all night, ears pricked for the jingle of money.

'They're arguing about their shares,' thought the old woman when she heard Colbert's voice singing '*Ayez pipitié d'elle*'. When she finally dozed off, she dreamt of a giant orange that grabbed hold of her and put her in its pocket, where it was dark and terribly cramped. There was a small hole in the pocket, and when she looked through it she could see all her money lying on the table in the banqueting room. There was a great pile of gold, silver, copper and banknotes, around which the guests were thronging. On the table next to the pile of money stood the notary, who was digging a coal shovel roughly into the pile and distributing the money all round. When he reached the last shovelful Madame Gendron woke with a start, got up and went unsteadily down to the banqueting room, which lay deserted in the early morning light.

And when Louise came out of the kitchen a little while later on her way to Richard's room, she saw the old woman still standing in the doorway and staring fixedly into the room.

From that moment Madame Gendron was bent on revenge. After thinking it over for a week she conceived the plan of creeping downstairs to the kitchen one night and turning on the tap, in the hope that the whole lot of them would drown.

The first plan, however, gave way to a second, whose object was the destruction of a huge clock that had been given to Madame Brulot as a wedding present and stood on the mantelpiece in the banqueting room. The ornamental dishes on either side had long been broken, but the central section had survived years of removals and cleaning ladies, and its mock gilt still gleamed like new. It included the clock proper and the decoration. The clock had a black face, but apart from that there was nothing very special about it. The decoration on the other hand was of very intricate design. The leitmotif consisted of vine leaves and bunches of grapes. To the right of the clock stood a shepherd and on the left the shepherdess, both of them carrying crooks and holding hands over the clock face; above the entwined hands soared a dove with a letter in its beak. In addition there was a mass of decoration that was less easy to make out, but all of which had a symbolic meaning. Well, Madame Gendron had set her heart on pulling this clock complete with its glass hood off the mantelpiece so that it smashed to smithereens on the floor of the room. However, there were serious snags attaching to the execution of this new plan. Firstly, the thing, standing there massive and immovable, looked so terribly heavy that the old woman doubted whether she would be able to shift it by herself. Furthermore she realized wisely – every now and then there was a surprising amount of logic in her train of thought – that the crash on the floor would make the whole house shake, that the maids and the guests would come rushing down to the banqueting room and she would be caught, found guilty and end up having to pay for everything.

Around this time it so happened that Chico had been particularly good one day, so that after dinner while they were having coffee he was given an extra lump of sugar. As always he sat on the shoulder of Madame Brulot, who broke off little pieces from a lump of sugar which Chico had to retrieve from between her teeth with his lips without using his hands. As she did this Madame Brulot closed her eyes and called him by the sweetest names a mother can think up for her child, such as:

> *Mon trésor*
> *Mon chéri*
> *Mon petit fils*
> *Mon Chico*
> *Ma Chicotte*
> *Mon petit rat*
> *Le fils à sa mémère*
> *Ma petite frimousse*
> *Ma grosse bébète*
> *Barberousse*
> *Moustache Polka*
> *Queue en l'air*
> *Mon petit cœur*
> *Ouistiti sapristi*, etc., etc.[26]

She also used occasional names like 'Clemenceau' when Chico had been particularly clever and 'Soleilland'[27] when he disgraced himself. The monkey answered 'cheep, cheep' when he took a moment's break from chewing, and together they made a noise like the cooing of two turtle-doves.

Madame Gendron had seen, heard and understood, and Chico's fate was sealed.

The old woman waited four whole weeks for the right moment to carry out the punishment. Finally, one afternoon, Madame had gone off to the Poor Relief Committee and Monsieur to his lawyer, and they had left the monkey at home, as it was too cold for him outside. Whenever Brulot and his wife both left the Villa without taking Chico with them, he was fastened by his chain to one of the legs of the sofa on which Brizard had died. He was tied up in such a way that the free length of chain allowed him to jump on and off the sofa to his heart's content, without being able to go so far that he was in danger of landing in the open fire while performing his acrobatics. Whenever the temperature was even a little below normal a fire had to be lit in the banqueting room to protect Chico from catching cold and dying. He could not stand the cold, however tough he might be in other respects. He would shiver so much it made one quite ill to look at him, and would bury his head between his shoulders like an old Capuchin monk. But even when there was no fire the creature could not be set free in the room, for Chico would break the glass-ware and knick-knacks on the sideboards, and given half a chance would leap into the garden and scramble up into the trees. No sooner was he perched up in the greenery among the branches than what little civilization he had picked up under Madame Brulot's tutelage deserted him and he reverted to being a true forest ape. Chico would swing fearsomely by his long tail and let his arms dangle like lady tra-peze artists do at the circus. He would go from one tree to another without touching the ground, and no one on earth could get him to come back down again of his own free will and join the people in the banqueting room. A hunt would be organized and led by Madame Brulot, involving the use of a lasso, chairs, ladders and a feather duster, in which hunt, besides Madame and Monsieur, the two maids and a few gallant gentlemen took part. Sometimes they were lucky, but more often than not it was hours before anyone managed to grab hold of the chain which hung down a couple of yards below the monkey and hampered his movements. One time Monsieur and Madame Brulot had given up the chase as hopeless at half past twelve at night and Chico had slept in the trees. Luckily it was a sultry night between two sweltering July days, otherwise it would have been the death of him. As it was, he got away with pneumonia, from which he recovered only very slowly. That is why Chico was tied to the sofa, and why there was still a fire in the banqueting room long after its human occupants had ceased to need one.

Madame Gendron had left the door of her room ajar, and had heard clearly when first Madame and then Monsieur Brulot had left. She had nothing to fear from the guests, for the old lady was not too senile to realize that they were all out at work or walking, depending on their situations. But there was some danger from the maids, as they might enter the room at any time to check the fire or poke around in drawers. Besides which, Monsieur and Madame Brulot might come back at any moment, and she would have missed her chance. So that the job had to be done quickly and efficiently.

The old woman went quietly downstairs and into the banqueting room, shutting the door behind her. Yes, there he was, on the sofa. He was carefully examining his tail with two hands. When he heard the squeak of the door he looked up and their eyes met. As though on command, Chico stopped his hunting and sat motionless, his hands still on his tail. The old woman too stopped for a moment, as it occurred to her that there was still time to call the whole thing off. But then in her mind's eye she saw Brulot and the four oranges again, and bore down resolutely on the monkey. The monkey seemed to realize that something awful was hanging over his head, for the moment the old woman took a step in his direction he gave a loud cheep, jumped to the floor off the arm of the sofa and crawled under it as far as his chain would allow. Madame Gendron walked around the table, crouched down, untied the chain and hauled the monkey, who was thrashing about like one possessed, out from under the sofa. When Chico saw that his premonition had not deceived him and that things were serious, he stopped chirping, went for the hand clutching the chain and quick as a flash made four little bite wounds in her thumb with his tiny teeth. But before he could take a fifth bite Madame Gendron's free hand had grabbed him from behind. Her big, bony fingers tightened round his throat and pressed his arms against his body. Chico screwed up his eyes fiercely and tried to scratch her with his hind legs, which were still hanging free. But the game was up. With a single swing of her arm the old woman tossed him into the fire. *Moustache Polka, le fils à sa mémère*, gave a shriek – just one – and stretched his arms above his head like the damned in hell in old paintings reaching out for Our Lord. He jumped up, supporting himself on his back legs on the glowing coals, but he could not see through the flames and the pain clouded his sense of direction. He leapt the wrong way, hit the wall and fell back on to the coals, where he remained. A smell of scorched hair filled the banqueting room.

Half an hour later Madame Brulot entered the banqueting room with her swaying step and, as she took out her hatpins with her arms above her head, she called out coaxingly 'Where is he? My little marmoset. He's going to have some su-su-su-su-sugar.' And she deliberately avoided looking in his direction, in order to tease him. When the hat had been deposited on the table and Chico still did not answer, she glanced at the sofa and around the banqueting room and then went to the kitchen.

'Did Chico go out with Monsieur?'

Louise thought for a moment, looked at Aline and they both shook their heads.

'Of course he didn't,' said Madame. 'It's much too cold anyway. But where is he then?'

'He must be in the banqueting room,' declared Aline, who suddenly remembered that she had heard the monkey chirping half an hour ago. That had been Chico's death cry, but Aline had thought that he was chirping for his own pleasure, as he often did.

Madame Brulot could not understand it, as she had found the door of the banqueting room closed. Just to be sure, she went and had a proper look, calling Chico by his sweetest names and again alluding to the sugar he would get if he showed himself.

At the hearth her eye was caught by the chain hanging out of the fire.

Madame stood there for a moment with a sick feeling in the pit of her stomach and her legs trembling. Then she wrenched the chain, which burned her hand, out of the fire. The other end was white-hot, and the jerking movement mixed Chico's ashes with those of the fuel.

Once Madame Brulot realized what had happened to her darling she started screaming.

Louise and Aline came rushing in and found her standing by the hearth with the chain in her hand.

'He's dead,' sobbed Madame.

'Who?' asked Aline, with just a glimmer of hope that it might be Monsieur Brulot she meant.

'Who? Who?' Madame burst out. 'How do you dare ask who? He's been burnt, dear God, burnt alive!'

'But, Madame . . .' ventured Aline.

'*Ah! laissez-moi!*' said Madame Brulot with a disconsolate gesture. Her grief commanded respect and the maids left her alone.

'And to think that I can't even have him stuffed,' she sobbed.

As the guests came home they were informed of Chico's tragic end by Madame, who did not tire of telling the same story over and over again. To make her account more vivid she put the chain back on the hearth and came into the room just as she had done at the time.

They all sympathized and had a few words of comfort for her in her distress.

Mademoiselle de Kerros convinced her that the impossibility of having him stuffed was a blessing in disguise. Her mother had an angora cat stuffed that she was terribly fond of. Pure white, with a long tail. But after less than a week she had had the stuffed creature buried in the garden because the sight of the motionless cat with its glass eyes had haunted her day and night.

'Yes, Mademoiselle,' sighed Madame Brulot, 'you're right really. And anyway, one doesn't have a child stuffed.' At other times she only very rarely addressed Mademoiselle, because as soon as it got busier in the Villa, Madame Brulot intended to ask her to move somewhere else, as she made such an unappetizing spectacle at table. And so as to soften the blow Madame kept her at a distance and tried to prepare her in advance by her silence.

Madame Brulot did not deign to say a word to the notary, who had left the monkey alone by the fire and so was responsible for what had happened, when he came in looking for all the world as though he had won his case. Madame Dumoulin, who felt sorry for him, put him in the picture with a few quiet words and a squeeze of the hand.

And Brulot, who was fully aware of the enormity of his crime, was dismayed and kept in the background, however difficult it was for him to keep quiet.

That evening at table they wore themselves out with a host of guesses as to the actual course of the drama, and reached the conclusion that the monkey had fallen in the fire by some accident and died as a result.

'Yes,' said Madame Brulot meaningfully, 'when grown-up people get senile and act like irresponsible children, then it's advisable not to keep pets.'

All of them, young and old, felt that blow beneath the belt, and all eyes were fixed on the notary, who acted as if he had spilt something and carefully brushed his waistcoat off. But the barb had hit home, for Brulot's goatee was quivering with pent up vexation.

'Let that be a lesson to you, my friend,' said Madame Gendron, and her words were filled with all the satisfaction that revenge can afford.

XVIII

Madame Charles

It was a nasty business, and Louise was constantly fretting and pondering on a way out. She had been *so* careful. She walked around talking to herself and examining herself in the mirror from morning till night, first from the front and then from the side, to see if she was already putting on weight. And even though nothing was noticeable yet, she imagined that everyone could see and that people were talking about it. She no longer wore starched aprons, as she thought that they made it worse, and she fastened her corset so tight that she could scarcely eat and sometimes had to push it down so she could breathe more easily. In the street she looked at all the women she met and only now did she see what an awful lot of them were pregnant.

Louise had not dreamt for a moment of telling Richard about her condition, for she was a real child of her people and was ashamed of admitting how inept a mistress she had been. She was also frightened of being a burden to him by worrying him with whining and nagging. The fact was that they had become lovers, and if she got into a scrape, physical or emotional, then it was up to her to sort it out. Louise knew that only too well. But still, Richard had noticed something was wrong, as he had already asked her a couple of times if she had a headache.

At first Louise had intended to let things take their natural course. But then she had seen herself in a dream as she would become, entering her village where her parents and Lucien were waiting for her, and her son not being able to help laughing at how fat she had grown. She also remembered the girl with the baby who had sat down on their park bench.

One evening when Madame had made a hurtful remark and

Richard had gone off to the German Club she had felt like drowning herself. She had already written a farewell letter, like the late Brizard, but at the last moment she had decided against it. Since Louise had left her village, and particularly since she had been on intimate terms with Grünewald, she seldom went to church. But now she had started to think about Our Lady again, and one Sunday morning she had gone to the chapel on the corner and bought three holy candles. It was a nuisance that she slept in the same room with Aline. Nevertheless she had lit one of the candles for three nights running and prayed to Jesus, Mary and her patron saint, St Louis, for help. And when Aline had inquired if she had gone off her head, she made up a story about Lucien having scarlet fever. But all her prayers were to no avail; she could tell, as she was hungry all day long.

Now that Jesus and his mother had abandoned her, she began thinking about one of those women. However, she lived in holy terror of them and so wanted to try taking something first. But not knowing quite how to go about it, and at her wits' end, she enlisted the help of Aline, who had lots of experience. It was a fortnight before she plucked up the courage to raise the subject. All that time Louise was especially nice and co-operative, helping Aline to clean the kitchen and deferring to her in everything. Finally, one evening, while Aline was standing at the stove with her back to her, Louise asked whether she knew of a good remedy. It was for a friend.

Aline replied that she didn't believe a word about the friend, that Louise really could trust her and that she knew of a chemist nearby who sold an excellent medicine. One had to say that it was for stomach-ache. It cost three francs, and two doses were enough. She also asked if it was 'the German's'.

That same evening Louise set off to get it. She waited across the street on a doorstep till there were no customers left in the shop. But then she saw a little boy, presumably the chemist's son, playing with a top between the two counters. Finally a man came out whom she took to be the chemist himself or an assistant, as he was bareheaded. He shielded his eyes with his hand against the gaslight and looked at the municipal clock which hung on the other side of the street. Then he went to fetch the shutters and started closing the shop.

Louise came forward, pulled the shawl she had put on right round her, and went into the shop.

'Mademoiselle?' asked the man, resting a long bar in the corner, which was used for fastening the shutters against the shop windows.

'Monsieur, I was told you have a good medicine for stomach-ache.'

Without looking at her the man reached under the counter and handed her a packet.

'Three francs. Bit chilly this evening, isn't it?'

Louise, who had the money ready, paid and left. Around the corner she opened the packet. It contained dried pine needles, or at least something that looked just like them.

With half the contents Aline made an infusion which had to stand all night. In the morning Louise had to take the brew on an empty stomach and not eat anything before the afternoon. If everything were not right after two days then she would have to try again with the other half.

Which is what she did. Louise put a lot of sugar in to take away the bitter taste and Aline, hands on hips, observed the whole process.

The medicine was no more effective than the praying had been, and now there was nothing for it but to go to one of those women. Aline knew of about five in the area, but seeing that Louise had no preference anyway, she should go along to Madame Charles on the boulevard Pereire,[28] as people spoke highly of her. As far as Aline knew, the going rate everywhere was twenty-five francs and fifty in more advanced cases. Louise was to say that she had been sent by her, as Aline got twenty per cent commission on all the ladies she referred to her. True, that only came to five francs in this case, but it was too much to throw away. But Aline did not want to profit at her expense and would give the money back to her. Madame could be consulted every day from two to four and in the evenings after eight. Payment was required in advance.

Louise was terribly apprehensive and made a private promise that she would donate Aline's five francs – provided everything went well – to the Mission for securing the release of Chinese babies, who otherwise were fed to the pigs by their mothers.

She decided to wait till Sunday, as she still wanted to spend a few pleasant days with Richard now it could no longer do any harm.

She went after dark, because the thought of going during the day upset her even more.

She felt sad.

The house looked perfectly ordinary, as did the whole neighbourhood, but it still made a very unfavourable impression on her and she sincerely hoped that she would not find Madame Charles at home. There were no name-plates in the hall downstairs, so Louise knocked on the concierge's door. The man was sitting eating.

'Madame Charles, please?'

'Fifth floor, third door on the right,' called the man without looking up.

Halfway between the fourth and fifth floors she met a young woman who did not look very well and was descending the stairs very carefully.

Louise thought 'she's just come from there', and said '*Passez*, Madame', backing against the wall to make way for her. The stranger passed her without a word and disappeared downstairs.

When she reached the third door on the right she was still hesitating. She looked through the keyhole but could not make anything out. Suddenly she heard someone inside coming towards the door. So as not to look foolish she quickly rang, and the door was opened by a pretty girl of around twenty who was about to go out.

'Madame Charles?'

'*Oui*, Madame. Won't you come in?'

The girl called out 'There's a customer for you', and left her alone.

Louise found herself in a bare room that was fitted out as a waiting-room. In the middle was a long table with a cloth over it, on which lay a red velvet album. On the walls were two signed portraits in gilt frames, of a man and a woman. Between the pair hung a crucifix, also gilt.

The door of the next room was pushed open, no doubt to discourage her from leaving, and Louise caught sight of the woman in the portrait, who was busy washing her hands with her sleeves rolled up. There was a smell of disinfectant in the air.

'I'll be right with you,' said the woman reassuringly.

A moment later she came in, drying her hands on her apron.

She was thin, but had an engaging face that indicated a good nature.

The complicated preamble which Louise had rehearsed once more while waiting turned out to be entirely superfluous, as Madame looked straight at her tummy. 'Please sit down, Mademoiselle. Just tell me how long it's been.'

'Two months,' said Louise.

'And have you tried anything already?'

Louise told her about the medicine.

'From that chemist in the rue de Longchamp, I suppose?'

She did not dare lie and said yes.

'Child, child!' cried Madame in gentle reproach, 'never bother with such things. It's all quackery. All it'll do is make you unhappy for the rest of your life. Take your hat off and come into the kitchen. It costs twenty-five francs and it's the usual practice in our profession for payment to be in advance. I trust you completely of course, as I can see soon enough what sort of person I'm dealing with, but that's just the way it is.'

Louise paid, glanced in the mirror and followed Madame Charles into the kitchen, which doubled as the operating theatre.

'I was sent by Mademoiselle Aline from the Villa des Roses,' said Louise, 'and she asked me to tell you.'

'Well, well. And how's she getting on? Is she still happy with her job? A good soul, Mademoiselle Aline.'

Madame Charles took a handful of green soap, put some water in a basin and began making a lather. Meanwhile she gave Louise a technical explanation of the advantage of the soap and water method, the only one she used. She had a horror of the surgical method and its devotees. What she did was the only proper way and everything else was dangerous. And she felt sorry for all those poor dears who fell into the clutches of some hag or other. So why did the soap and water method have so few advocates? Very simple, because with soap and water one was never sure of succeeding first time and often had to start all over again twice, three, even as many as five times. And those creatures reckoned it was too much trouble for twenty-five francs, that was all there was to it. Laymen didn't appreciate these things, but she'd been in the profession for almost twenty years and knew what she was talking about.

When it was all over, Madame Charles saw her out. If nothing had happened within three days, then she must come back. And if she was not home then Louise would be helped by her daughter, who was already amazingly good for a girl of nineteen. Louise could rely on her completely too. Finally she sent her regards and thanks to Aline. And if ever any members of her family or friends of hers were in a fix, then she was to send them along and she would get the same commission as Aline.

'Well?' asked Aline.

'Well, I don't know yet,' said Louise.

She had to go to Madame Charles's another four times and each time Louise found her a little less friendly when she asked 'Still nothing?' She now regretted having paid the whole amount in advance, instead of, say, half.

Thank God, after the fifth visit she was finally able to take to her bed.

XIX

Mrs Wimhurst

A lot had happened at the Villa in the last few days.

In the first place the postman had brought an announcement of a death which had been taken for a circular and had fallen on the floor unread. When Madame Brulot came upon it by chance a few days later while looking for a scrap of paper on which to make a laundry list, it turned out that Monsieur Maurice Victorien Dupuis, after a long and painful illness, had passed away at the age of seventy-three years and six months. Maurice Dupuis was the owner of the Villa des Roses.

'I say, have you seen this?' Madame Brulot asked her husband.

'Well, well,' said Brulot. 'So old Dupuis is dead. A ripe old age.'

Madame Brulot rushed off a letter of condolence to the family, and soon afterwards received a visit from Monsieur Bernard, the late Monsieur Dupuis's agent, who came to collect the rent every three months. He had hoped that the Dupuis children would leave everything as it was and that they would continue to show the confidence in him that the old gentleman had done for so many years. And they probably would have, seeing as they had all been dandled on his knee, but the youngest son, who had got into debt with gambling and living it up, did not want to keep his funds tied up in property a moment longer and now they were on the point of selling off the Villa to a construction company, which would be certain to demolish the house and put up a block of flats in its place. It was pure speculation. The construction company in question knew only too well that sooner or later the avenue Carnot would be lengthened and seeing that the narrow rue d'Armaillé was the continuation of the wide avenue, the whole street was bound to be compulsorily purchased at some point in the future.[29]

And was a compulsory purchase order a good deal for the land-lords? You bet it was. If they held on to the house it would triple in value in less than ten years. He had explained the whole thing, but there was no reasoning with that raving lunatic Georges. The upstart had even told him, Bernard, to shut his trap or he could get out there and then. Which of course meant that he would not last much longer, whether he kept quiet or not. That was the thanks he got for going old and grey in the service of the Dupuis family.

Everything happened just as Monsieur Bernard had said it would, and a fortnight later Madame Brulot had already had notice that the Villa would have to be vacated in a year's time.

It was a severe financial blow, for there were sure to be no more houses to let in this neighbourhood for the derisory rent she had paid the late Monsieur Dupuis. Furthermore it was doubtful whether her lodgers would come with her, because such people often do the craziest things and one cannot rely on them. But worst of all was the fact that no one would know her new address, while at the old Villa des Roses there was a constant stream of new lodgers, even if Madame Brulot did not advertise in the papers or put herself out in any other way to attract custom. It was true that there were not that many, but they kept on coming from far and wide and of their own accord. And when Madame occasionally asked how they had come by her address, then the names of people were mentioned who were total strangers to her. Aasgaard, for instance, had come from Christiania to Paris carrying a piece of paper in his pocket with 'Villa des Roses, rue d'Armaillé' clearly written on it. He had been found in the street looking for the place with the piece of paper in his hand. He could give only the vaguest indication of how he had come by the document, and as far as could be deduced from what he said, an uncle and some other people must have been involved. And the Villa had similar obscure connections not only with the far north, but also with most other countries, even with Peru and the Balkan states. Of course the *clien-tèle* had increased the 'commercial value' when Madame Brulot had taken over the Villa.

And all that was now going down the drain and she would have to begin again from scratch, just as she had sixteen years ago when she had come to Paris with the old notary in tow.

Marie and her mother had stayed on at the Villa for a week after Madame Dumoulin's party, and for all that time, with Madame Brulot's permission, Louise had taken them a portion of the food which was left over from the banqueting room and was returned to the kitchen. The two women did not dare show their faces for the first couple of days, and, while Marie hunted for a position in town, her mother hid in the room. She only came out to fetch the food which Louise placed discreetly on the floor outside the door of the room, and to creep to the toilet in the early morning or late at night when everyone was asleep. And when she needed to relieve herself at an inconvenient time, she sometimes waited for hours till she had a chance to get to the maids' toilet unnoticed.

Marie had already offered her services as an office girl, a hair-dresser, a pedicurist, a stage extra, a ladies' companion and a photographer's model. But for all these jobs she was either too old, too clumsy, too unqualified or too fat, depending on the nature of the business. She was also entirely without references.

Once she had imagined she saw Martin, but it was not him.

Finally, after a week, when the mother started appearing in the hall again and both of them, for the first time since Martin had left, had slept till the afternoon, Madame Brulot got Louise to tell them that the room had been let and they must leave the Villa the following day, before dinnertime. Well, it could not go on indefinitely. At the request of Mademoiselle de Kerros, Colbert sang a song at lunch and took up a collection which raised eleven francs twenty.

So they left. Marie carried a full hatbox and a fur stole over her arm, her mother a large parcel. They left the trunk behind because that could not be transported free.

Shortly after Marie and her mother, the youngest of the three Hungarian ladies had also left, to move in with an uncle. She now wore splendid outfits and lugged a lapdog about with her. Three or four times a week she collected her sisters from the Villa in a car in the afternoons to take them out for a drive.

So business had not been going too well for some time and Madame Brulot was dejected. First Martin's flight, then the tragic death of Chico, then the news that she would have to move, and finally the departure of the young Hungarian girl, who would be sure to see to it that her sisters soon acquired uncles too. And for four months there had been no gain to offset this apart from Mrs Wimhurst. A mere trifle, since she had left the Villa after only two days. Later, when her new business had been set up, Madame still enjoyed telling the story of how she had acquired the trio. She had read an advertisement in the paper from an American lady, informing all interested parties that she was intending to come to Paris for six months with her two-year-old son and a nanny and was looking for rooms in a 'smart' family boarding-house. Madame Brulot, not having the remotest inkling that her Villa would not possess in full measure the required degree of smartness, asked Grünewald, who was said to know English, to write a letter to the London address given. So Grünewald, with the help of an Englishman who worked in his office, composed a splendid letter, which was lovingly sealed and posted, and a few days later a telegram arrived: 'Arriving tonight ten o'clock. Prepare rooms. Wimhurst.' Madame was so delighted that she gave the messenger boy a double tip and asked Grünewald to stay home that evening to act as interpreter.

And so Mrs Wimhurst was awaited in the banqueting room by Richard, Madame Brulot and Monsieur Brulot, who was wearing his black cap and a jacket which still had some of Chico's hairs clinging to it.

At half past ten a carriage drew up outside the door and the American woman entered. Young Wimhurst Jr. was asleep and was carried by the nanny.

Mother Wimhurst had a slim, attractive figure and as far as one could tell in the poorly lit hall she was wearing an elegant travel outfit. Richard put her age at twenty-eight.

As she crossed the threshold she seemed to hesitate for a moment as to whether she should go any further. She took her lorgnette and examined in turn Monsieur Brulot, Madame Brulot and the walls of the vestibule. But the old notary seemed to interest her especially.

'Villa des Roses?' she asked.

'At your service, Madame,' said Brulot, nodding and making a jovial gesture intended to convey the message 'make yourself at home'.

Grünewald helped fetch the cases from the carriage.

Madame Brulot lit a candle and showed Mrs Wimhurst to her room, up the same spiral staircase which was used by Madame Gendron, Mademoiselle de Kerros and Mr Knidelius.

The further they went the greater the astonishment of the American lady seemed to become. When they got upstairs Madame Brulot put the candle on the washstand, pushed down on the bed so that the resilience of the spring mattress could be seen to its best advantage, and threw back the blankets to show that the sheets were clean and that no one had slept in them. From the adjoining room came the hoarse voice of Mademoiselle de Kerros, who was obviously in high spirits and was drumming on the table by way of accompaniment, as she had no piano upstairs.

'Is this my room?' asked Mrs Wimhurst in English, taking up her lorgnette again.

'She wants to know if this is her room,' translated Grünewald, who arrived lugging a heavy suitcase.

'Room?' replied Madame Brulot. 'Yes. All for you and baby. Maid separate room.'

'Oh, I see,' said the American lady.

Then she asked Richard to ask Madame Brulot whether she and the maid could have something to eat at this hour. The reply was that there was something ready in the banqueting room, and would they like to come downstairs. Baby, who slept through it all, was put to bed.

Supper passed in silence and, after Mrs Wimhurst and her maid had appeased their hunger, they retired upstairs. When they got upstairs again Richard asked the beautiful American woman whether there was anything else he could do. She replied that she could manage the rest herself and handed him a two-franc piece as a tip for bringing up the valise and unloading the cases. Richard refused the money politely and explained that he was not a servant but a guest like herself. This made Mrs Wimhurst laugh, and for the first time she observed him closely. All things considered, Richard was a good-looking fellow.

'Listen, sir,' she said, 'you'll appreciate that I can't stay in this house. There's been a misunderstanding. Would you mind helping me to thank the woman downstairs for the trouble she has taken and at the same time ask her to prepare my bill?'

'Certainly, Mrs Wimhurst,' said Richard, 'with pleasure. The moment you came in I saw that the Villa was no place for you.'

He now told her the story of the letter, without mentioning the Englishman who had corrected it. Finally he advised her to stay on for a few days, so that she could look round at her leisure for a *pension* more in keeping with her position. He would be glad to assist her in this if she agreed. Mrs Wimhurst decided to follow this good advice and thanked Richard for his helpfulness with a heavenly smile.

The following afternoon Richard asked for time off from his office 'on serious family business', and they set out together. Mrs Wimhurst wore the most elegant clothes and it was a pleasure to walk around town with her, as many gentlemen turned to look at her. A suitable *pension* was soon found, after which they went for tea and cakes together at a first-class *pâtisserie*. The American lady paid for everything. She told Richard that her husband, who had stayed in America, was deceiving her, that she did not care about him any more, and that she took a bath every day. Once she was in her new *pension*, Richard must come and visit her now and again, because she did not know a soul in Paris and did not like being on her own.

The next day she left the Villa and the very same evening Richard spent his hard-earned savings on a fashionable suit, a panama hat, a high double collar and a slim walking-stick, for his visit to Mrs Wimhurst the following Sunday.

XX

Richard's Departure

The maids' room was separated from the street by the kitchen and from the garden by the room which Martin and his ladies had occupied. It was a dreary place. Even in the afternoons it was almost dark in there, as the only daylight came from a small window let into the kitchen wall high up near the ceiling.

This was where Louise had gone to bed, after the fifth visit to Madame Charles. She lay by turns on her left and right side and on her back, and was given lemon water by Aline, of which she took the occasional sip.

Morning, afternoon and evening she listened to Richard's footsteps and on the second day she heard him ask Aline if she were nearly better yet.

However reluctant Louise might have been to tell him what was really the matter with her, she still found it a shame that in his eyes it would all pass off as an ordinary bout of flu and that he would have no suspicion of how she was paying for her love with a fever and violent abdominal pains.

Aline, who also realized that it was hopeless for Louise to lie there suffering under such circumstances, could finally no longer just stand by and say nothing. And when Richard came into the kitchen again on the third evening, this time to ask if there were any letters for him, she replied, with a nod of her head towards the room where Louise was in bed, that 'there had been a letter in there for the last three days dying to be collected' and that he was a 'rotten cad'. Richard asked her to explain herself more clearly, whereupon she blamed him for everything in a string of abuse.

Grünewald looked at the door, asked her to keep her voice down a bit, and claimed to know nothing about anything. Louise had told him all along that she had a headache.

This was too much for Aline. She crossed her arms indignantly and assured him solemnly that he could thank his lucky stars that he was not dealing with her. Whereupon she started brandishing her saucepans so furiously that Richard no longer felt safe in the kitchen and retired to the banqueting room. Aline, meanwhile, found him more attractive than before, after his affair with Louise.

Grünewald was far from happy at the thought of what the consequences might have been if Louise had not decided to do what she had done. Still, the incident had given him a certain satisfaction and at table, in the banqueting room, he had looked at the ladies triumphantly as if to say 'just you behave yourselves, or you'll be next in line'.

After dinner he paid Louise a visit. He put his cigarette on her bedside table, pulled up a chair and sat down at the bedside. It was already so dark in the room that the patient could no longer be distinguished from her pillow. Louise held out an arm, pulled him to her and they embraced. The bedclothes felt clammy and there was a smell of vegetables in the room which came from the kitchen.

'Do you still love me?' she whispered.

Richard shrugged his shoulders.

'Of course I do. Otherwise I wouldn't be sitting here, would I?'

'Have you got a new suit on?' inquired Louise, her curiosity aroused. She could not make out anything in the darkness, but when she put her arm round him, she had felt tweed, and he did not have even one tweed suit.

'Don't you worry your head about that,' said Richard, who was thinking of Mrs Wimhurst, 'just you make sure you get better soon. By the way, Louise, why did you keep all this from me? Wasn't I worthy of your confidence?' He picked up his cigarette again.

'Oh,' she said, 'it's all over now anyway.'

Richard sat there for a little while and then lit the candle to see what time it was. Louise quickly brushed the hair out of her face and pulled the covers up to her chin.

'Has Monsieur got a rendezvous?' she asked laughingly.

'Yes I have, as a matter of fact,' said Grünewald, and he made up a story about a new job he had his eye on. 'Make sure you're not late then,' said Louise.

'It's all right if I stay another five minutes,' said Grünewald reassuringly.

In the candlelight everything became clearly visible. Louise did not look at all well, lying there.

'Haven't I got thin?' she asked.

'Not very,' said Richard. 'I think your features have got more delicate.'

'Don't talk rubbish,' said Louise. But it pleased her.

'What's that?' asked Richard.

'Lemon water.'

'And that?' pointing to a package wrapped in newspaper lying on the bedside table.

'Nothing,' said Louise, reaching out for it.

But Richard beat her to it.

'What do you mean, nothing?' he asked curiously and tried to open it.

'Richard! Leave it done up! Then I'll tell you.' She sounded so stern and at the same time so afraid that he did as she said.

In a few words he knew everything.

'I think we should get rid of it,' said Louise.

'You're damned right we should get rid of it, *Donnerwetter!*' replied Grünewald sharply, 'and the sooner the better! How terribly careless of you.'

He put it in his coat and got up.

'Can I do anything else for you?' he asked.

He gave her a kiss, wished her a speedy recovery, blew out the candle and left her alone.

It was a simple funeral: he went to Mrs Wimhurst's *pension* by a roundabout route and, on the way, in a deserted street, threw the package with the thing in it over a fence.

A few days later the patient was on her feet again, and when Richard was unable to make a date with Mrs Wimhurst for the following Sunday, not daring not to go out with the convalescent Louise, he started thinking about leaving the Villa des Roses.

The matter was soon decided, as Louise lost out to the other woman on all counts. With the American woman one could show oneself in the street and in company, while Louise carried with her everywhere the ineradicable stamp of her humble origins. Besides, Mrs Wimhurst was slimmer, suppler and yet fuller-figured. And she had caressing fingers and delicate hands, while Louise's wrist joints were so thick that she could not get her bracelet over them. Moreover, Louise had lost one of her eye-teeth, so that a gap showed when she laughed.

Richard rented a room in another neighbourhood from the beginning of the following month, and a few days later informed Louise and Madame Brulot of his impending departure. He was going to spend four weeks with his parents in Breslau, after which he would be returning to Paris; and it went without saying that he would be coming back to live at the Villa des Roses. Louise said nothing, and with an apprehensive feeling she helped him pack his case at the end of the month. She could not help thinking back repeatedly to the words of Perret, 25 rue Servette, Genève, who had said 'Do not give in to the blond one', and she regretted having confessed to her brother that Richard was her lover.

But when she went walking with him again on the last evening, she felt new hope, because he calmly downed large glasses of beer and generally acted so normally. He even sang her a song.

They said goodbye by the chapel on the corner where they had stood that first evening. She was crying, but he told her to keep her spirits up and patted her good-naturedly on the shoulder.

The following afternoon a man came with a cart to collect the cases, just as had happened with Brizard. To be on the safe side Richard had brought a burly friend from the German Club with him, as one never knew. They stood talking German in the hall by the kitchen door, and Louise listened. But all she knew was *'ich liebe dich'*, *'eins zwei drei'* and *'bis zum Tode getreu'*, and none of those came up in the conversation.

The cases had gone, and the friend stood brushing the dust from his hat while Richard took his leave of Monsieur and Madame Brulot and the guests. Then he came to the kitchen to say goodbye to the maids.

Aline, who was at the sink, gave him her little finger to shake so as not to make his hands wet and asked if he would send some post-cards, which he promised to do.

Then he shook hands with Louise as well, and left.

Monsieur Brulot, Madame Brulot and Aasgaard stood on the front step and each time he turned round raised their arms above their heads.

Aline watched him go, through the window, humming a familiar tune, and when he had disappeared from view she clicked her tongue as if to say 'that's that'.

Louise sat in the corner of the kitchen, resting her elbows on the table and covering her face with her hands.

'Maybe he'll come back,' said Aline, by way of consolation.

'Oh, shut up, Aline,' replied Louise.

It was warm that afternoon, and, as Richard was bored in his office, he had a moment of weakness. He was still so young. He sent Louise a parting note, intended to give the impression it had been written before he boarded the train. It began 'Darling Louise' and ended with 'I love you so.'

XXI

The Retreat

After Grünewald's departure Louise went on living and working without saying a word to anybody, and Aline found her insufferable. She cried a lot, had almost no appetite, and her hearing became poor. She also had kidney trouble. Madame Brulot found her less efficient than she used to be and criticized her every day, particularly since Aline, after a quarrel with Louise, had told her the whole story. Yes, she now remembered all kinds of details she had formerly paid no attention to.

'I'd never have believed such a thing of that girl,' said Madame Brulot to her husband.

'Never trust those little saints,' replied the old notary.

And Madame Gendron, through no fault of her own, had to atone for the German, as Louise washed her less gently than before, and when she was done on one side turned the old woman over with a rough gesture.

So the four weeks passed and many others after them.

Louise wrote him a letter which received no answer. Shortly afterwards she wrote two more in quick succession.

'He's let himself be turned against me,' she thought. 'Maybe they're keeping him locked up.'

As Richard had seen more of Aasgaard than of the other guests, she began to suspect the Norwegian and spied on his comings and goings with hostile looks. But that shed no light on things and now she tried to get round him with sweet talk.

But when at the end of six months she had still had no word from Richard, she finally had to admit what Aline had already told her a hundred times.

Her indignation was as great as her grief, and she decided to save up until she had enough money to go and track him down in Breslau.

It was quite a feat for her to plan an itinerary, as she had never been further than Rambouillet, which was less than an hour on the train. The railway timetable, with its masses of figures and its map which did not have Breslau on it, drove her to distraction. Day after day she sat leafing through it for hours and the more she looked the more it made her head spin.

One day when Aline was nice to her for the first time since the quarrel, Louise told her what she intended to do. But Aline said that they did not understand French in Germany and that she was in danger of being eaten by bears and other wild animals in the forests. She knew all about it, as she had once seen it on the stage. Louise wavered a little, but refused to be put off, and, when she went on insisting, Aline took the timetable and looked in her turn. She had once been to Rouen with her mother ten years or so ago and that had been quite a journey too. They soon found Rouen on the map, and Creil, where another aunt of Aline's lived who had lots of money and was divorced, but there was no sign of Breslau.

'Shall I tell you something,' said Aline, 'I don't think there's any such place.'

But still Louise did not give up, and when, a few weeks later, a railway van pulled up outside, she asked the delivery-man who brought in a package for Madame Brulot if he knew where Breslau was. The man asked her to repeat the question and then replied that he did not. But when Louise explained that it was a town somewhere in Germany, he advised her to inquire at the information office of one of the main stations.

The following Sunday she set off. Knowing no better, she went to Sceaux station, from where she took the train to her village. However, there was nobody in the information office except a man who was dusting. She thought that to knock would be rather rude, and so she stood at the window till she was spoken to. When the man saw that she was not going to go away, he came up with a frown and asked what she wanted.

Louise replied that she would like to know how to get to Breslau, whereupon the man with the duster said that the clerk had gone to lunch and would be back in an hour or so. Louise thanked him and went for a walk. After three-quarters of an hour she came back and took up her position at the window.

Finally a man in an office coat appeared and asked her what she wanted.

Louise replied that she would like to know how she could get to Breslau.

'What town did you say?'

'Breslau.'

'Breslau, Breslau,' repeated the chap, peering out of the window. Then he took a thick book out of a cupboard, opened it and began looking, going up and down the pages with his index finger.

'Ha!' Louise heard him say.

'Madame, you must go to the inquiries office at either the Gare du Nord or the Gare de l'Est. Maybe you can go from either, but if I were you I'd go to the Gare de l'Est first. I think that's your best bet.'

Louise thanked him and went to the Gare de l'Est, which was an hour and a half's journey.

She waited at the window till a man looked up from his books and asked her what she wanted.

Louise replied that she would like to know how to get to Breslau.

'You'll be going third class?'

'Yes, Monsieur.'

This man also opened a book, looked for a long time, went over to ask advice from a colleague who gave him a playful dig in the ribs, and came back to where she was.

'We only issue tickets as far as Chemnitz and that costs 90 francs 30 return. Change at Heidelberg, Würzburg and Nuremberg. Departs at 10.15 in the evening.'

'And when I get to that town, Monsieur?'

'Chemnitz? They'll put you right there. You'll get a ticket to Breslau from there of course. There'll be an information office there.'

'And from there to Breslau, Monsieur? How much is that?'

The man did not know, but no more than fifty francs return, he thought. In Germany there was a fourth class too.

'Thank you, Monsieur. Where was it I had to change again?'

'Heidelberg, Würzburg . . . wait a minute and I'll write it down for you,' said the man, as Louise had quite a nice face.

He brought a sheet of paper and wished her a pleasant journey. Louise thanked him again and left. On the stairs she unfolded the note and read:

Paris (Est)	dep.	10.15 pm
Carlsruhe	arr.	10.32 am
Heidelberg	arr.	11.29 am
	change	
	dep.	12.28 pm
Würzburg	arr.	4.54 pm
	change	
	dep.	5.04 pm
Fürth	arr.	6.48 pm
Nuremberg	arr.	6.58 pm
	change	
	dep.	8.47 pm
Bayreuth	arr.	10.42 pm
Chemnitz	arr.	4.08 am

Change and get ticket for Breslau.

'Four changes,' she reflected glumly.

Meanwhile time had not stood still and the day finally arrived when Madame Brulot felt obliged to inform her guests that the Villa would have to be vacated in a month's time. She was determined to start up a new boarding-house, but as yet she had not found anything that suited her. As soon as she had, however, she hoped that she would be able to number all the ladies and gentlemen among the *clientèle* of her new establishment. They would be able to find her new address in *Le Journal*, in which she would place an advertisement three or four Saturdays in a row, when everything was fixed.

Some sooner, some later, the guests left the Villa. Aasgaard and Mademoiselle de Kerros had left a few months before – Aasgaard because his leave was over and Mademoiselle de Kerros because, since the Norwegian's departure, she had suffered from epileptic fits and got up to the oddest things. Also she could no longer be tolerated at table, as the blotches on her neck had become so bad that she wore a shawl the whole time, even when it was warm. The two remaining Hungarian ladies moved into Sweet Home and Knidelius had left without saying where he was going.

Madame Brulot had thought about keeping Madame Gendron with her and taking her along to the *pension* where she would be living with the old notary till she had set up her new business. They could all get by on the old girl's eighteen francs, and Madame Gendron could easily pass as Monsieur Brulot's mother or something, so that the landlady would not even suspect that she was putting her up at second hand.

Madame Gendron's son, however, had other ideas, and a few days before the end of the month he came to collect his mother personally in a carriage and take her to another *pension*. He had closed the deal by letter from Dunkerque, agreeing on a price of twelve francs a day, and he wanted to go and introduce her.

When the lady at the new *pension* saw the old woman, she commented that the correspondence had mentioned an 'elderly' lady, but that she had not for one moment imagined that Madame would be so old and decrepit.

'You're exaggerating,' the son assured her, 'Mother is still quite able-bodied.'

'One wouldn't say so at first sight,' observed the woman.

'You don't think so? Well, you'll be pleasantly surprised.'

And turning to his mother he said loudly, slapping his thighs to make himself clearer:

'Walk about a bit, Mum.'

Mum got up and started walking up and down the room, from where her son and the landlady were sitting to the far wall and back again.

'Enough, enough,' said Gendron, stopping her with a laugh, since the old woman did not seem inclined to sit down again of her own accord.

'Well, what do you say to that, Madame?'

'Yes,' said the landlady sourly, 'that's not too bad. But what about up and down stairs, Monsieur! And my stairs are quite awkward.'

'Stairs, steps, you name it and she'll get up them. Isn't that right, Mum, that you can get upstairs perfectly well by yourself?'

'Yes, dear,' said Madame Gendron.

'*Enfin*,' said the woman, 'we'll give it a try. Then I'll be in touch with you about it.'

The widow Antoinette Dumoulin rented a room somewhere and ate in restaurants till such time as Madame Brulot's new establishment was ready, because she certainly did not want to move to another *pension*, however difficult it might be having no one to talk to at mealtimes.

As for Madame Brulot, by the end of the month she had still not found a suitable abode. So she put the furniture in storage and went with the notary to live at *pension* Belle Vue for the time being. So that after seventeen years of running the Villa, they found themselves lodgers. Out of habit Madame Brulot continued to note everything that went on, and when something or other was not up to scratch, she would nudge the old notary with her elbow. And Brulot would shake his head and say: '*Quel service!*'

Now back to Louise.

For her the imminent vacating of the Villa came as a heavy blow. If only she could stay where she was, waiting for him, till she had money enough to go to Breslau. But now! What if he returned, with who knows what honourable intentions, and came and looked at the place where the Villa had been, while she was back in her village and so knew nothing about it! And if in a few months' time she were to embark on her journey while he was combing all Paris for her!

So she decided to have one last try at mollifying him in writing, before she had to go to Chevreuse, and wrote the following letter:

My darling Richard,

   I can't sleep tonight and have come to talk to you again, as that is my only consolation, without much hope but because I can't forget you. This is already the fourth time I've written since you left, but I've still had no answer.

   Let me tell you first how I'm getting on, although I know it doesn't matter very much to you. I'm ill and having trouble with my kidneys and in a lot of pain. Shortly after you left I tried to move Madame Gendron's bed all by myself, because of the vermin, you know, and with the strain of lifting a kidney detached and now I'm being treated by the doctor. Madame Brulot is annoyed to see me poorly and says it's my own fault, as I should have called Aline to help me. And on top of that I'm sad and weepy all the time. She would have got a new chambermaid long ago, but it's no longer worth the trouble of changing, as the Villa is due to be pulled down in a fortnight's time. Still, she's good to me in other ways, because she pays for the doctor. She goes on at me for misbehaving in her house, everyone points the finger at me and Aline gloats over my misfortune. On the slightest pretext she says, 'Well, what about your fine Richard now? He's jilted you good and proper!'

My God, I wish I were dead, that would be the best thing for it. I loved you too much, Richard. But sooner or later you'll be sorry or it'll be your turn to suffer what you've made me go through. Oh, you're so rotten to me. If it goes on like this, I'll get to the point where I put an end to my suffering. And I've got a little son that I love *just as much* as you. But he's being well looked after there, because they can afford it. Well, they'll just have to adopt him, since they've not got any of their own, and then I'll know for sure that he'll never go short of anything.

Why didn't you come back, Richard? I begged you to in all my letters and if you don't do it right away now, it'll be too late, because I have to leave here at the end of the month. But if you should come back later, then you can write to me at my father's address, c/o M. P. Carton, Chevreuse, Seine et Marne, France.[30] The letter will reach me there or else they'll have to forward it to Paris if I've found another position here in the meantime.

Darling Richard, I intended to come and visit you in Breslau. I pleaded with Monsieur Aasgaard and threatened him, but he would not tell me anything. 'I don't know anything,' he tells me, because he's a liar too. But even though I'm stupid, I've found everything out. I have to leave from the Gare de l'Est and change at Heidelberg, Würzburg, Nuremberg and Chemnitz and the fare is one hundred and fifty francs return third class. It's just that I haven't got enough money, which is why you haven't seen me in Breslau yet. But you needn't hope you'll never see me again, because you might be disappointed. If I'm not out of work for too long, I'll have got together about two hundred francs by the end of the year.

Darling, we shall see each other again, I swear it. We were everything to each other for five months and for me they were like years. And to think you had the nerve to sing 'La Douce Colombe' to my face, the evening before you left. And do you remember, in the forest of St-Cloud, what you taught me there? 'Faithful unto death!' Richard, you won't easily forget the year that's about to begin. I'm doing my best to keep going, with all my sorrow and misery. The doctor has told me to wear a surgical belt and I shall live cheaply and save and crawl to you on my hands and knees and one day you'll find me on your doorstep, dead or alive.

I have too much trust in your goodness to be able to bear the separation which you secretly planned and brought about, and I freely admit that I had good reason to doubt and stand there crying when you told me that one lover always loves *most deeply* and that one was you. You've certainly proved it! 'My darling Louise, I love you so much,' it says in your last letter by postal tube that I sit and read every night. Oh, how you deceived me!

Richard, I'm really not angry with you. Come back soon or write me a letter, till the end of the month at the Villa and after that at my father's address, c/o M. P. Carton, Chevreuse, Seine et Marne, France. Don't think I'm doing this in order to get married to you or anything. No, Richard, don't be afraid, but let's be like we were before. I ask no more of you.

I embrace you a thousand times. Write soon.

Your broken-hearted
LOUISE
71 rue d'Armaillé

Grünewald had sent instructions to the postmaster at Breslau, so that he received all these letters in his new boarding-house, only fifteen minutes' walk from the Villa des Roses, where the heavy-hearted Louise sat watching and waiting in vain till the end of the month. When finally nothing had come, no Richard and no letter, she packed up her things and went back to her village. 'I should have sent Perret the sheet that looked like a burning candle,' she thought.

She arrived at about midday.

She walked slowly from the station to where her parents lived and as she came to the first houses was overtaken by a friend who had been to school with her and was pushing a wheelbarrow.

'Well, well, if it isn't Louise. And how's Paris?' said the woman scornfully, as country folk do when they talk about the city.

'Fine, Marie, fine,' answered Louise, tight-lipped.

She looked up the road and saw the baker's shop and the white lettering above the door of the post office.

It was her village sure enough.

Rotterdam, 1910

Notes

1. The rue d'Armaillé and the Quartier des Ternes are located in the west of Paris, in the 17th *arrondissement* (see map).
2. The reference is to the Franco-Prussian War.
3. Née Jeanne Antoinette Poisson, 1721–64.
4. Alphonse de Lamartine, 1790–1869.
5. An abbreviated Dutch patronymic ('son of C . . .').
6. '(That includes) as much wine as you like.'
7. Chevreuse and Rambouillet are situated some 20 km and 30 km south-west of Paris respectively, in the *département* of Yvelines.
8. 'It's very sad. He's made a big mistake.'
9. A café with live music.
10. There is a chapel (St-Ferdinand) at the corner of rue d'Armaillé and rue St-Ferdinand (see map).
11. Present-day Wrocław, in Poland.
12. 'THE FUTURE FORETOLD. Love. Marriage. Fortune. Inheritances. ADDRESS FOR CONSULTATIONS . . .'
13. 'May God be with you!'
14. 'I have a presentiment.'
15. 'Yet you know very well, Richard, that I'm not a bad woman, the kind you pick up in the street.'
16. 'Torture by expectation'.
17. 'Have pi-pi, have pi-pity on her.' ('Pipi' is children's language for 'pee'.)
18. '. . . and so shrivelled up,/One would take them for a pair of Brussels sprouts . . .'
19. 'This is the story of Madame Gendron . . .'
20. 'In this gloomy place,/So full of dread,/What is that phantom/That is always there before me?'
21. 'Your forehead so pure wore a crown/Made of the flowers of the days of your youth.'
22. 'God, reject this criminal soul,/That was false to its word and its faith.'

23. A village on the western outskirts of Paris, with a large park overlooking the Seine.

24. 'I love you', 'one two three'.

25. The avenue de Wagram runs north-east from the place de l'Arc de Triomphe (see map).

26. 'My treasure. My darling. My little boy. My Chico. My Chica. My little rat. Mummy's little boy. My little sweet-face. My big baby. Barbarossa. Moustache Polka. Tail-in-the-air. My little sweetheart. Marmoset mischief.'

27. Georges Clemenceau (1841–1929), French statesman, Prime Minister of France 1906–09. Soleilland: this allusion to a notorious serial sex murderer active in Paris before the First World War, which had mystified Elsschot scholars, was finally identified by Ronald Spoor. Spoor's article 'Elsschots aap uit de mouw' appeared in *De Parelduiker* 97/1, pp. 66–69.

28. The boulevard Pereire is a major artery of the Quartier des Ternes (see map).

29. The avenue Carnot was in fact never extended (see map).

30. There is no locality of this name in Seine-et-Marne, though there was in the pre-1964 *département* of Seine-et-Oise. This could be either a slip or poetic licence.

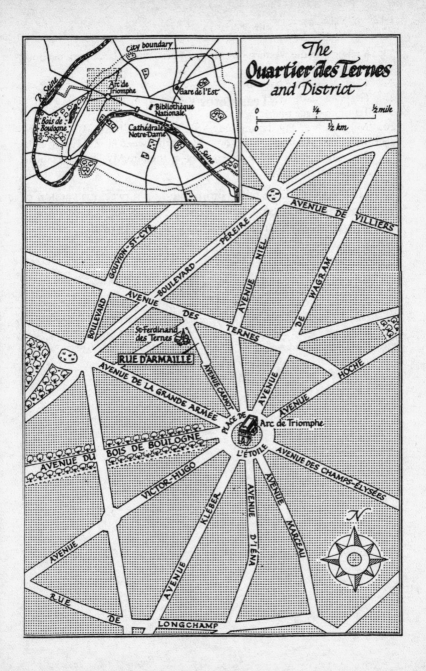

The Quartier des Ternes and District

City boundary

R. Seine

Arc de Triomphe

Gare de l'Est

Bibliothèque Nationale

Bois de Boulogne

Cathédrale Notre-Dame

R. Seine

0   ¼   ½ mile
0   ½ km

AVENUE DE VILLIERS

GOUVION · ST · CYR

BOULEVARD PEREIRE

AVENUE NIEL

AVENUE DE WAGRAM

BOULEVARD

AVENUE

DES TERNES

St Ferdinand des Ternes

RUE D'ARMAILLÉ

AVENUE CARNOT

AVENUE HOCHE

AVENUE DE LA GRANDE ARMÉE

AVENUE

AVENUE

PLACE DE L'ÉTOILE

Arc de Triomphe

BOIS DE BOULOGNE

AVENUE DU

AVENUE DES CHAMPS-ÉLYSÉES

VICTOR · HUGO

AVENUE KLÉBER

AVENUE D'IÉNA

AVENUE MARCEAU

N

AVENUE

RUE DE LONGCHAMP

Translator's Note

I wish to thank all those who commented on a previous version of this translation, and especially Vernon Pearce for his astute and helpful remarks. Remaining imperfections are my own.

Cheese

Willem Elsschot

Translated by Paul Vincent.

Frans Laarmans is a humble shipping clerk. One day he is suddenly elevated to the position of chief agent for a Dutch cheese company, with responsibility for Belgium and the Grand Duchy of Luxembourg. Thrilled at the change in his status, he goes on leave and sets up an office at home. He takes the order of ten thousand full-cream Edams.

But running a business is not as straightforward as he thought. As the bulk of the twenty tons of cheese sits in storage, it starts to haunt him. And when his employer wires him to say he is coming to Antwerp to settle the first accounts, Laarmans begins to panic . . .

'Enchanting, a little gem' Deborah Moggach

'A comic masterpiece' *London Review of Books*

Taking it to Heart

Marie Desplechin

Translated by Will Hobson.

At once wickedly funny and unexpectedly touching, Marie Desplechin's debut collection of short stories explores life and love in contemporary Paris. Here are the trials and tribulations of sex in the city, as – with alarming frequency – her heroines' affairs fail to measure up to their expectations. They're not asking for much: but how much is too much? How long should they wait? And what should they do in the meantime?

Sweet, sharp and unsentimental, Desplechin's stories capture eight unlikely moments of truth.

'Marie Desplechin has an incredible ability to reveal the extraordinary in everyday life' *Elle*

'Cool, clever, funny and deeply contemporary' *Big Issue*

The Ugliest House in the World

Peter Ho Davies

'The Ugliest House in the World is in North Wales, in case you were wondering, where a broke young doctor has gone to visit his father in the wake of a local boy's accidental death. The remaining seven stories in this distinctive, highly crafted collection focus on small-scale desperation set in a variety of locales – including Coventry, Natal, Patagonia, Southeast Asia . . . Whether you're reading about a grieving father searching for redemption by working at a crisis line, or eavesdropping at an officers' dinner during the Boer War, you'll be transported to another, highly affecting world' *Guardian*

'Every word slots into perfect place in a debut that puts not a foot wrong' *Mail on Sunday*

'Wherever these globe-trotting fictions go, vaulting across continents and swerving through time lines, their humour, poignancy and understanding is never far behind' *Sunday Times*

Don't Look at Me Like That

Diana Athill

In England half a century ago, well-brought-up young women are meant to aspire to the respectable life. Some things are not to be spoken of; some are most certainly not to be done. There are rules, conventions. Meg Bailey obeys them. She progresses from Home Counties school to un-Bohemian art college with few outward signs of passion or frustration. Her personality is submerged in polite routines; even with her best friend, Roxane, what can't be said looms far larger than what can.

But circumstances change. Meg gets a job and moves to London. Roxane gets married to a man picked out by her mother. And then Meg does something shocking. Shocking not only by the standards of her time, but of our own.

'She has added importantly to those works of literature which illuminate the vagaries of human emotion' *Daily Telegraph*

When I Lived in Modern Times

Linda Grant

Winner of the Orange Prize for Fiction 2000.

It is April 1946. Evelyn Sert, twenty-years-old, a hairdresser from Soho, sails for Palestine, where Jewish refugees and idealists are gathering from across Europe to start a new life in a brand new country.

In the glittering, cosmopolitan, Bauhaus city of Tel Aviv, anything seems possible – the new self, new Jew, new woman are all feasible. Evelyn, adept at disguises, reinvents herself. Immersed in a world of passionate idealism, she falls in love, and with Johnny, her lover, finds herself at the heart of a very dangerous game.

'A novel that both stimulates the mind and satisfies the heart' *Scotland on Sunday*

'Beautifully written, passionate . . . a deeply felt song of praise for Tel Aviv' *Sunday Times*

Moth Smoke

Mohsin Hamid

Pakistan, Summer 1998: hot, with a late monsoon and the occasional nuclear test. In Lahore, Daru Shezad loses his job. While the jet set parties behind high walls, the economy crumbles and Daru's electricity is cut off. Soon he has fallen for his best friend's wife, started mixing heroin with his hash and joined forces with a criminal rickshaw driver. *Moth Smoke* is the story of Daru's spectacular downfall: a bittersweet tale of politics and corruption, of friendship and betrayal.

'A vivid portrait of contemporary young Pakistani life, where frustration and insecurity feed not only the snobbery, decadence and aspirations of the rich, but also the resentment of the poor' *The Times*

'Like the moths of the title, burned by their attraction to a naked flame, Hamid's characters find it hard to resist the urge to self-destruct. And this tale might just burn you, too' *The Face*

A Gesture Life

Chang-rae Lee

A Gesture Life is a haunting, compelling exploration of the Japanese experience of the Second World War, and the fate of their 'comfort women'.

'You make a whole life out of gestures and politeness,' Sunny tells her adoptive father, Franklin Hata. Franklin deflects everyone with courtesy and impenetrable decorum, becoming a respected elder of his small, prosperous American town.

As Sunny tries to unpick her father's scrupulous self-control, the story he has repressed emerges: his life as a medic in the Japanese army and his love for a Korean woman forced into sexual service of the troops.

'A wonderful mixture of Richard Ford and Kazuo Ishiguro' *New Yorker*

'Stunning . . . It's a beautiful, solitary, remarkably tender book' Andrew O'Hagan

'A writer of immense subtlety and craft' *Guardian*

The Mezzanine

Nicholson Baker

The Mezzanine is the story of one man's lunch hour. It addresses the big questions of corporate life in the grand manner:

Why does one shoelace always wear out before the other? Whose genius lies behind the wing-flap spout on the milk carton? Whatever happened to the paper drinking-straw?

'A seriously funny book. Things (shoelaces, drinking straws, earplugs) will never seem the same again' Salman Rushdie

'*The Mezzanine*'s ambitions are as grand as its obsessions are small, and out of that disparity comes a refined and engaging chatter strung about with great jokes. It's also useful, full of debates about paper towels and putting on socks . . . Andy Warhol would have loved this book: he would have bought 2,000 copies, just for a laugh. Everybody else should make do with just the one' *Independent*